Bewilderment

of

Boys

a novel

To Philip
With love & light
Karon Luddy
February 14, 2015

Karon Luddy

Cover photograph by Erin L. Hubbs

Library of Congress Cataloging-in-Publication Data

LCCN: 2014903810

Luddy, Karon.

Bewilderment of Boys /Karon Luddy.—First edition.

ISBN-13: 978-0-9915518-0-4 (pc)—ISBN-978-0-9915518-1-1 (ebook)

FIRST EDITION

Backbone Books

.

For anyone who has ever been
or ever will be
seventeen

For Grayson and Genevieve Bowman,
the grandest of teenagers

To the memory of my mother
Frances Robertson Gleaton
September 3, 1924—April 15, 2013

And to the memory of
David Bryan Faulkenberry
June 15, 1955—June 14,1968

The earth is crammed with heaven.
Elizabeth Barrett Browning

I was saying to myself, or perhaps praying, "Why can the world not permit two lovers (any two) a moment of escape, free of all its claims, to be in love, just the two together, each other's all?"
Wendell Berry

Be not afraid then to read my appeal; it is not written in the heat of passion or prejudice, but in that solemn calmness which is the result of conviction and duty. It is true, I am going to tell you unwelcome truths, but I mean to speak those truths in love.
Angelina Grimké

Contents

PART I

Zealot

The sphinx must solve her own riddle.

— Ralph Waldo Emerson

CHAPTER 1

Lonesome Creek

The higher I rise, the more the porch swing wobbles, but I do not care. It's high noon Saturday, the seventh ridiculous day of August, and my skinny, freckle-faced twin brothers have gotten on my last nerve, driving their homemade go-cart in the driveway—impersonating the Apollo 15 astronauts they saw on TV a few days ago zooming around on the moon in that fancy lunar roving vehicle. I can't believe I agreed to watch them just so Mama and Gloria Jean could go to the S & H Green Stamp Store in Columbia to buy a crib for a two-month old zygote. You'd think Gloria Jean was incubating the New Messiah, the way she and Mama go on about it.

A rainy smelling wind blows across my face, and I look up and see a trio of storm clouds bunched together in the East. Damn it all to hell—I forgot to hang out the laundry. Mama will have a conniption if she doesn't have any clean underwear tomorrow. I rush inside, take the clothes out of the washer, plunk them in the basket, and carry them to the clothesline out by the garden. I hang six pairs of Mama's white cotton panties, three of those pointy-tipped cotton bras she orders from Sears, and her pale yellow slip, which looks halfway sexy quivering in the breeze. Next, I pull out Mama's new Lycra girdle and place a clothespin on each side. It hangs there stiff and sinister like a Garment of Torture. Mama's got a good figure. Why she wears this contraption is beyond me.

A few pieces of laundry are left in the bottom of the basket—they look like handkerchiefs in pastel colors. I pick up a mint green one. It's one of those little cotton dresses I wore when I was a baby—the casual, unfrilly kind Mama keeps in the cedar chest and is now handing down to Gloria Jean. I hang the tiny dress with two clothespins that look gigantic—then hang the others: pink, yellow, blue and white. The dresses dance in the breeze as if inhabited by little baby ghosts.

I walk around the house and sit on the front porch step. Noah's still pushing Josh around on the lunar vehicle. Being around those nitwits makes me feel like I've been on this earth two thousand years. Maybe a drive in the Sleeping Elephant will help un-mutilate my nerves. I walk inside, grab the keys off the knickknack shelf, and put them in my pocket. Mama's ceramic figures are coated with a fine layer of dust—so I lift my T-shirt and wipe off the tiny blue turtle, gawky American eagle, cocky matador and his fuming bull. Then there's that family of black poodles held together by gold chains. I wipe off all five of them and go outside.

The twins jump into the backseat of the ancient gray Plymouth station wagon Daddy handed down to me after he bought the red Fairlane. I back the car out of the driveway and ease down the street. The breeze feels good blowing across my cheeks and the smell of gasoline makes me feel dizzy and happy. There's hardly any traffic on Highway 200. Shift change at the mill isn't until four o'clock. I pass the Jiffy Grill and Red Clover Second Baptist that has *All Things Must Be Done Unto Edifying* spelled out on its sign. I love that word *edify*—it's a snappy sounding word that means to improve someone's knowledge so they can behave better.

On the radio, Janis Joplin taunts some man to come on and take another piece of her scrumptious heart, as if a taste of it would send him straight to heaven—which is where I hope Janis found herself after she overdosed last year. That hoarse screaming voice of hers makes me feel like there's a whole wide crazy world out there calling me. But then a vision pops into my head of a little red-haired girl running toward me hollering *Aunt Kawleen! Aunt Kawleen*—and she looks just like my sister Gloria Jean. Good God Almighty! I am SEVENTEEN years old—too young to have a niece—especially one who pronounces my name wrong, like the twins used to do. Crazy laughter wells up inside of me, but I clench my teeth to squelch it.

I turn into the parking lot of Mickey's Bait & Tackle Shop, a small cinder block building painted baby-shit green.

"Can we go with you?" Noah asks sweetly. "Pl-e-e-eze?"

"No. I'll be right back."

A cardboard sign is duct-taped to the tattered screen door: *Night Crawlers, 75¢ per dozen.* Inside, my eyes try to adjust to the dim light. I've been in here hundreds of times with Daddy, buying crickets, worms, and minnows, Zero bars, M&M's and Pepsis, but I've never been in here alone. Today, there's no one here but Billy Ray's mama, who's reading a book behind the counter, looking happy as can be since she got up the gumption to leave her husband Crawdad, who has a terrible case of the can't help its.

Teeny looks up, waves, and goes back to reading her romance novel. Mickey's is a combination grocery story, bait-shop, and restaurant. At shift-changing times, it's usually packed with men from the mill sitting on upside-down minnow buckets, smoking cigarettes, chewing tobacco, gobbling boiled peanuts and pickled eggs, and farting and belching like nasty boys. Daddy and I used to spend most Saturday evenings here at Mickey's—before the twins plopped into the world eleven years ago. I loved listening to Daddy and his buddies talking about fish they caught. I didn't know any of the men—so my mind worked overtime—imagining where they lived, what their wives and kids were like, and what kind of parents they came from.

Remembering those innocent days makes my heart feel like a busted up accordion. I wish like hell I could paint like Marc Chagall—I'd fill up a canvas with Mickey's darkness as the background and paint Daddy's and those other men's faces all aglow telling their fish stories.

I grab two bags of M&M peanuts and put them on the counter. Teeny's nose is still stuck in *Lonesome Creek*, probably reading about how Jenny Giggleton is getting some forbidden love from Gerard Manley Hopkins Junior. Lonesome Creek must be one hell of an intriguing place. I clear my throat. Teeny looks up and slams the book shut. "Hey, Karlene, just candy today?"

"Yes, ma'am." I hand her a dollar.

"Bet your mama's excited about becoming a grandmother," she says, eyes twinkling like dying stars.

"Happy as a clam."

"I can't believe that boy of mine is all grown up and in the Navy."

"Ditto," I say and walk outside.

I toss the M&M's to the twins in the backseat and drive toward town, but there's a big turtle making its way across the road, its neck stretched to Kingdom Come. I ease off the gas and roll to a stop. Pretty damn convenient to carry a geometrically perfect house on your back—but an image of its cracked bloody shell flashes in my mind. I get out, pick up the turtle, and set it down on the parched lawn of the fairground. I drive to the library and park.

The twins tumble out of the car. I hand them two dollars each.

"Pick you up at Kelly's in a little while."

They race down High Street, and I stroll up the steps to the library. Miss Sophia's little clock sign indicates she'll be back in thirty minutes.

I lift the key from under the flowerpot and unlock the door. Sunlight streams through the tall skinny window onto the gargantuan dictionary perched on its mahogany throne—my favorite oracle. I turn to a random page and run my finger across the paper until there's a buzz of energy. My finger rests on the word *ROMANCE*—the *last* thing I need to think about, but I read the first three definitions:

- *a ballad of adventure in love and war*
- *a composition expressive and sentimental in character*
- *a narrative of a wandering knight*

The only narrative bugging me these days is about a wandering *sailor* named Billy Ray Jenkins. To distract myself from the idea of romance, I walk to the magazine rack and pick up the latest issue of LIFE dated August 8, 1971, with the headline: *After Ten Years, Big Success for the Sex Kitten.*

Underneath is a close-up of Ann-Margret that shows off her bountiful cleavage. But that reddish blond mane of hers looks as if King Kong has run his fingers through it. Her weary smile and jaded eyes tell me her sex kitten purring days are over. Poor thing looks nothing like the healthy happy girl, who danced with Elvis in Viva Las Vegas. I shove the magazine into my tan leather book-satchel and write a note:

Dear Miss Sophia,

I'm looking for information about the Grimké sisters from Charleston, who denounced slavery back in the 1820s. I'd love to get my hands on any correspondence you can find of theirs. Might help me with that application to Smith College.

Your acolyte, Karlene

p. s. I borrowed the new issue of Life.

I walk next door to Independent Savings & Loan, then prance to the counter like I own the place. "Hey, Mrs. Crenshaw, you sure look classy in those new wire-rimmed glasses," I say, to the cute teller whose husband was blown to pieces in Vietnam last year.

"Glad you like them—they cost a fortune."

"Worth every penny." I pull a check from my pocket and hand it to her. "Please deposit this into my get-out-of-Red-Clover, S.C. fund."

She flashes a lopsided grin and examines the check. "Good Lord, how much are the Harrisons paying you to babysit—twenty bucks an hour?"

"I'm more like a nanny, and that check is for the month of July."

"They pay you well."

"Probably because I am so good at my job," I say bragging.

"Figured as much," she says, handing me the receipt.

We say adios, and I walk next door to Red Clover Hardware and peek inside the window. Three teenaged boys stand in line holding bolts or screws in their sweaty palms. Every one of them struck dumb by Lucinda Randall, who's working the cash register in a bright green smock—their brains conjuring up images of her strutting around in her red-sequined majorette costume that shows off her impressive breasts, tiny waist, and sexy behind. Since Billy Ray left for the Navy, Lucinda's been trying to get me to change my scholarly ways and participate in her favorite sport, which she calls the bewilderment of boys, but I've always treated boys just like girls—befriending the ones who have a mysterious aspect to their personality. Lucinda says I need to quit reading those highfalutin Ralph Waldo Emerson essays and taste the luscious fruits of this world—but Mama's been pointing me in an entirely different direction since the day I was born. But Lucinda's too busy with her boy-bewildering, so I walk two blocks to Flower Power Records.

The musky scent of patchouli discombobulates my senses, and Bob Dylan's voice oozes out of the speakers like the Undertaker of Love—coaxing some girl to get into his big brass bed. Lucinda's brother walks toward me, his auburn hair pulled into a ponytail, and hands me the *Tapestry* album by Carole King. "Your boyfriend sent the money and asked me to get this for you."

"I told you, I don't have a boyfriend." I say, preferring not to discuss Billy Ray Jenkins with Spencer Randall.

"Whatever you say, Champ," he says, rolling his eyes.

I look at the cover, admiring the photograph of Carole with long curly hair sitting on a windowsill with a fat tabby cat.

"Carole King is a great songwriter—even inspired me to write a few."

"Mind singing one for me?"

"You sure you want to hear me sing?"

"I'd love to hear you sing."

"Okay, you asked for it." I belt out the words in a singsong voice:

> *Zealot for you baby*
> *dreaming of your touch*
> *trying to figure out why I*
> *love you so much.*
>
> *When we first kissed*
> *I thought I would die—*
> *but I spread my wings*
> *and started to fly.*
>
> *You've owned my heart*
> *since the day we met*
> *I promise our love will*
> *never bring regret.*

The befuddled look on Spencer's face makes me feel like a plucked turkey, so I quit singing. "I know my stupid song sounds like a stupid cheer."

"No, it does not. Sounds like you're halfway singing and halfway talking like Johnny Cash. When did you write it?"

"I don't remember," I say, lying.

"Mind telling me how you wrote the lyrics?"

"I don't know—they just came to me."

"Well, where do they come from?"

"I have no earthly idea."

"Where did it FEEL like they came from?" he says, eyes dancing.

"Sometimes lyrics brood in my heart. Sometimes they pop into my brain, but this one started in my epidermis."

"Epidermis?' His eyes bug out like a cartoon character.

"Yes, epidermis. E-P-I-D-E-R-M-I-S. A perfectly good word," I say, adrenalin rushing through my bloodstream. He slaps his leg and laughs until he's into a full-fledged guffaw with tears streaming down his face.

I stand there with my hands on my hips, fuming.

He stops laughing and lifts his t-shirt to wipe his face, exposing his torso that looks like Michelangelo chiseled it. My eyes can't help but to feast on his manliness.

"I loved your song," he says apologetically.

"So that's how you show your love, braying like a donkey?"

"Sorry for getting hysterical. Got my draft letter this morning—lottery number was 77. Uncle Sam done got himself another soldier puppet."

"What are you going to do?"

"Thinking about enlisting in the Air Force—cutting a better deal—I should have gotten my ass into college two years ago instead of playing music with the Weevils."

"You followed your dream—nothing wrong with that," I say, glossing over the fact that his daddy ran off with Darla what's her name, and left his family without a dime for groceries, much less a penny for college.

"Maybe I followed the wrong dream."

"Your dream to make music is NOT wrong."

"And your song is NOT hilarious," he says.

I stand there looking at Spencer, my mind awhirl with images of five other Red Clover boys who got drafted—every one of them under nineteen—and every one of them dead. Too young to vote. Too young to drink. None had ever been on an airplane until Uncle Sam flew them to Southeast Asia for the sole purpose to kill or be killed.

"Sorry about you getting drafted," I say, hugging the *Tapestry* album to my chest. "Maybe we can hang out later tonight."

"I'd like that, but I have a gig in Columbia."

"See you later." I saunter out the door and cross the street.

Kelly's standing on the sidewalk in front of Royal Taxi—carving a bear from the trunk of our black walnut tree that got struck by lightning. Most people stress me out, but Kelly is real as dirt. When he's not transporting folks around town or whittling animals out of wood, he sponsors my daddy. Without him, I would never have known what it was like to have a sober father. I wait until he finishes sharpening the bear's claw. "Hey, you old coot."

"Hey Miss K, what you doing loitering around town?"

"Trying to remain sane."

"Well, you in the wrong place for that."

"Thou knowest what thou speaketh of."

Kelly grins, his black skin crinkling around his caramel eyes. "You look perturbed. Something bothering you?"

"Everything is bothering me."

"Maybe it's the drought," Kelly says.

"The drought is NOT my problem. My problem is my sister's belly is swelling like a hot air balloon, and Spencer Randall just got drafted—which is wrong in ten thousand ways."

"It's insane," Kelly says, shaking his head.

"Speaking of insane, have you seen the twins?"

"They're up at the square, playing with their new yo-yos."

"See you later, Mister K." I sashay toward the courthouse in my cutoffs, tossing my dark blonde mane like the girl in the Summer Blonde commercial.

Across the street, Spencer sits on the old church pew outside the record store, wailing away on his black Les Paul guitar, singing that old blues song he likes so much in that deep soulful voice of his: *I got a letter this morning, how do you reckon it read? It said, "Hurry, hurry, yeah, your love is dead.*

CHAPTER 2

Dear Holy Spirit of Mary

Around six o'clock that evening, Mama comes into the kitchen with mail in her hand—her face glowing like a woman who just bought a crib for her future grandbaby. "Twins give you much trouble?"

"The usual amount," I say, dropping spaghetti into boiling water. "Did you and Gloria Jean get the baby crib?"

"Sure did."

"Why didn't she stay for supper?"

"Wendell's taking her out to eat tonight," she says, handing me an envelope. "Here's a letter from Furman University."

I tear open the letter and start reading it.

"Come on, tell me what it says," she says all chirpily.

"It's from Dr. Geoffrey Bannister, Dean of Admissions. Someone recommended me as an outstanding scholar, and he'd like for me to visit their campus within the next few weeks to discuss the possibility of a scholarship for next fall."

"Congratulations, honey. You sure don't take after your mama— I'm dumb as an iron skillet. I can barely read my own writing."

"Sit down Mama and hush. There is not one dumb cell in your whole body. Besides, a lot of geniuses have scribbly handwriting."

"Don't mind me, I'm just having myself a pity party. What I need to do is go to night school and earn my high school diploma. Gloria Jean and Wendell keep bugging me about it."

"You'll get around to it." I knead the knotted-up muscle on the right side of her neck. Mama's good at lots of things, but she never cuts herself any slack, especially about dropping out of high school in eleventh grade.

"I need to count my blessings instead of worrying myself into a migraine."

"What you need to do is lighten up on yourself," I say, trying to imagine my feet in Mama's shoes. Last year, she had her uterus and ovaries removed at High Memorial Hospital. Now she's going to be a grandmother—another major adjustment. And next fall, I'll be leaving for college. She acts happy about me going away, but after Gloria Jean married Wendell four years ago, Mama moped around for six months.

"Thanks for the rub, but I feel like there's thirteen hammers banging in my head. Nothing to do but get some rest. Will you make sure the boys get to bed?"

"Yes, ma'am."

"And don't forget to call Mrs. Harrison about the letter from Furman. She'll be tickled to hear about it."

"Okay. How about some spaghetti?"

"No thanks, honey." She walks to our tiny bathroom and shuts the door.

That closed door makes my calves knot. I know she's worked up a migraine, but if I have to baby-sit the twins tonight, I might flush the turdlings down the toilet. I drain the spaghetti, turn the sauce on low, and walk outside. Noah and Joshua are replacing the tire on their fake lunar roving vehicle. They look hungry and dirty, but not nearly tired enough. I hold up a quarter. "The first person to run around the house five times gets it."

They nod and take their positions.

"On your mark. Get set. Go."

Joshua darts out in front of Noah, racing full out. I sit on the porch step, pick up a stick, and start writing adverbs from *Lady Chatterley's Lover* into the red clay dust. Since Lucinda insisted I read the confounded book, I've noticed how fond D. H. Lawrence is of adverbs—the fancier the better. I scribble *lugubriously* into the dirt—a five-syllable word that means sadly. I wipe it out and write more adverbs as they pop into my head: *lustily*, *tragically*, *aesthetically*, *passionately*, *persistently*, *disastrously*, and *constrainedly*, which is ironic as hell because of how constrained I feel about everything.

Until I opened *Lady Chatterley's Lover*, I had never seen the "f" word written in a book. Old D. H. Lawrence used it 26 times. He also ranted and raved about what he called the Bitch-Goddess of Success, mentioning her 18 times—talking about how vile she smelled and how hungry she was for flattery. I don't know why he personified success as a female. Why not Bastard-God?

"Yeehaw," Josh yells as he turns the corner, running side-by-side with Noah.

"Final lap!" I yell, stretching my arms wide, making myself the finish line.

Joshua leaps into the air like Superman and slaps my hand, then tumbles into the red clay dust. I flip the winning quarter to him. Noah's face contorts with rage, so I slip him a Hershey's kiss before he starts acting like a jackass. We go inside. The twins eat two platefuls of spaghetti, take their baths, dive into their bunk beds, and flop around like dying catfish for a while before finally falling asleep. I check on Mama. She's asleep, her foot dangling off the bed.

I call Mrs. Harrison and tell her about the letter from Furman and she offers to go with me next week. Then after a long hot bath, I watch the last five minutes of *Gunsmoke*. Miss Kitty is tending bar at the Long Branch, playing hard to get, but Marshall Dillon is so wrapped up in his sheriff's job, he doesn't seem to notice, which is the main thrust of the show. Two people in love, walking around in different circles, with a total failure to communicate.

I trudge to my room, close the door, and stretch out on white High Cotton Mill sheets. My yellow shorty pajamas feel tight all over. It's so hot I can barely breathe. An image of Spencer's muscled torso flashes in my mind—making me feel all hot and bothered by it ALL—but my inner neon H--A--L--T sign starts flashing— reminding me to use the acronym I learned in Al-Anon. I ask myself the four questions:

Am I **H**ungry? No.

Am I **A**ngry? Partially.

Am I **L**onely? Maybe.

Am I **T**ired? ABSOLUTELY.

Remembering this H-A-L-T acronym might keep me sane.

Might as well reflect on my day using Step Ten: *Continued to take personal inventory, and when we were wrong, promptly admitted it.* Daddy taught me a trick on doing this step. It's not so much about WHAT you did—but rather HOW you did it. And thanks to D. H. Lawrence's adverb fetish, I came up with a short cut: *Think of an adverb that describes my attitude about what I did.*

I pull out my notebook, make a list of activities, and select an adverb that describes how I did it.

Babysat the twins—Furiously.
Hung out the laundry—Meticulously.
Saw Billy Ray's mama—Achingly.
Sang Zealot song to Spencer—Foolishly.
Cooked supper—Dutifully
Gave Mama a pep talk—Compassionately.
Got twins to bed—Aggravatedly.

Reading over my list, I realize I did a whole lot of stuff that needed to be done, which makes me feel like a halfway decent human being instead of a sex-crazed songwriting nincompoop. I didn't mean to sing the stupid song for Spencer—I wrote it for Billy Ray. A prayer never hurts, so I move on to Step Eleven: *Sought through prayer and meditation to improve our conscious contact with God, as we understood Him, praying only for knowledge of His will for us and the power to carry that out.* I ignore the masculine pronouns and address God as I understand *Her.*

Dear Holy Spirit of Mary,

I guess you know about my skin-tingling encounter today when Spencer lifted his shirt—and I guess you know he's been drafted. And I guess you also know I am terrified of becoming an aunt. If I weren't so tired, I'd take a walk in the moonlight and stroll down to Bear Creek and baptize myself in your name. I really appreciate how you understand me—always telling me to be kind to myself. You understand the deepness of being a woman, with ovaries, breasts, and a womb. When your spirit enters me—my heart beams bright as the beacon in Lady Liberty's hand standing out there in New York Harbor. I really appreciate the way you flash divine thoughts into my mind every once in a while. And I appreciate the opportunity to visit Furman with Mrs. Harrison. But please note I'm home alone, all by my self, again, on Saturday night. I'm seventeen years old, not a spinster. Aloha, Adios, and Amen.

My new *Tapestry* album catches my eye, so I put it on my Zenith record player and turn the volume low so it won't wake Mama. Carole pounds out a dozen or so notes on the piano, then sings about how every time her boyfriend comes around the Earth moves and her heart starts trembling. A perfect way to start a song—with a big burst of life. I sing along: *Ooh Baby—Ah Darling* and how our emotions cannot be tamed—no way—no how.

CHAPTER 3

Ivory Tower

D
r. Bannister swirls in his black leather chair and motions out the window to the enormous white tower rising from the grassy peninsula that juts into Swan Lake. "That bell tower is the finest ever built in South Carolina, but Furman's president deserves all the credit. When he discovered the Citadel had sixty-nine bells in their tower, he raised enough money to hang seventy bells in ours. We are proud of our tower, Karlene, and we are proud of our school."

"And you should be, sir. I am very impressed by what I've seen today, but the idea of attending a college associated with the Southern Baptist Convention makes me queasy."

A bemused smile spreads across his face. "Queasy, how so?"

"You see, sir—for the past seventeen years, I have been associated with Southern Baptists, and I can assure you my candor has not been appreciated. Baptists believe in obedience and doing things the way they've always been done, but I believe that as individuals, we should develop our personalities to the highest degree."

"Preacher Smoot didn't mention obedience in his recommendation letter. He pointed out your persistence, wit and intelligence," he says with a hearty smile.

"Preacher Smoot is highly tolerant for a minister. He and I have been discussing this Father, Son, and Holy Spirit business for years, much to my mother's chagrin. Mama is profoundly Baptist and believes the Bible is set in stone. But Preacher Smoot always listens to my point of view, even though he rarely agrees with it. And he's rabid about me getting a scholarship here at Furman."

"Herbert and I were roommates in college—rabid describes him perfectly," he says, tweaking his red bowtie. "Now tell me, who is your all-time favorite hero?"

"Reverend Martin Luther King, Jr. When I read his *Letter From a Birmingham Jail*, I felt like a red tailed hawk soaring above all the world's problems. The way he chastised those phony-baloney clergymen, who blamed him for stirring up white folks, is a perfect example of how to approach ignorant individuals—with aplomb and grace. Education is a slow process, sir. Slow as molasses. South Carolina has a couple of centuries of work left to do in the civil rights department. It was our secession that started the Civil War. We owe it to ourselves to finish the work Dr. King started. There are lots of troubled hearts in South Carolina. We need to alleviate as many of them as we can."

"Ah yes, troubled hearts. Goes right along with Furman University's motto: *Christo et Doctrinae*. You know what that means?"

"For Christ and Learning," I say in a robotic voice.

His eyebrows form little teepees. "You have a problem with that motto?"

"No sir, I have enormous respect for Jesus. The story of his life is the most enigmatic and transcendental I've ever read. It breaks my heart the way his life built to that one penultimate moment on the cross at Calvary—when he told God to forgive his crucifiers. Jesus did not ask God. He told God to forgive them. That's what I call courage. Just like when Jesus was twelve-years old and his parents scolded him about being at the temple without permission. Jesus told them they had no say-so in the matter. But years later, when his mama told Jesus they needed wine for the wedding at Cana—he listened to her. Jesus could have turned that water into buttermilk if he'd wanted to, but his mama asked for wine, so that's what he gave her. It also turned out to be his first miracle."

He smiles like a doting disciple. "Speaking of miracles, I heard you got a private tour of the White House after you won the spelling bee. Did anything in particular grab your attention?"

"Yes sir, the portrait of George Washington that hung above the fireplace in the Oval Office. The reverence in his eyes and the way his hand was tucked inside his jacket close to his heart touched me. When I returned to Red Clover, I studied President Washington's first inaugural speech, and discovered that he wrote about God in an intimate way, without once using the word God. He used figures of speech such as 'Almighty Being who rules over the universe,' 'Great Author of every public and private good,' 'Invisible Hand which conducts the affairs of all life,' and my personal favorite 'Benign Parent of the Human Race.'"

"I love that metaphor—Great Author of every public and private good."

"I like it too, Dr. Bannister, but what really caught my attention was President Washington's candor. He tells the American people they had caused him enormous anxiety by electing him as their president—and their confidence in him forced him to take a good hard look at himself, which made him aware of his own deficiencies. His humility made me curious to make a modern day comparison, so I studied Mr. Nixon's inaugural speech. He mentioned the word God six times, but used no figures of speech and no presidential sounding words, such as vicissitudes, predilection, immutable, auspiciously, or tranquility." I stop right there before I pontificate myself into a stupor.

Dr. Bannister's pen races across the page.

Nobody wants to hear that scholarly gobbledygook.

I need to lighten up.

Finally, he looks up. "Sounds like Washington, DC inspired you."

"Yes, sir, but I had fun, too, hanging out with my friends, Tommy Ludinksy from New Jersey and Janine Whitehead from Kansas City, and seeing the Lincoln Memorial. But the grooviest thing was swirling around in President Nixon's chair in the Oval Office, and Ollie, the White House photographer taking a photo."

"Groovy, indeed. What other schools interest you?"

"My former spelling coach, Mrs. Harrison, is set on me going to her alma mater, Smith College. They have this Native Daughter Scholarship program she wants me to pursue. However, Mr. Harrison wants me to go to his alma mater, Clemson. It's a fine school too."

"Any university would be lucky to have a scholar like you."

"Thank you, sir. If Furman University offers me a scholarship, I promise to give it every consideration."

"If you do decide to come here, please stop by for a frank discussion now and then," he says, then stands and offers his hand.

"Indeed, I will," I say, shaking it firmly.

Dr. Bannister escorts me to the lobby. Mrs. Harrison beams like the Flying Nun. They start chitchatting, so I excuse myself and stroll outside feeling content as a just-burped baby. Maybe the Christian atmosphere at Furman is exactly what I need. But those seventy bells start clanging in the tower—a song that sounds like a victory march and funeral dirge melted together. Makes me think about how the

Southern Baptist Conference refuses to ordain women, saying a pastor has to be the *husband of one wife.*

Why in the world can't they ordain the *wife of one husband?*

And it's beyond me why the president of this fine university took on the petty project to hang one more bell in their tower than the Citadel had in theirs, but when it comes to football rivalries, even highly educated Baptists act like nincompoops.

CHAPTER 4

Nothing but a Heartache

On the outskirts of Gaffney, Mrs. Harrison steers her Country Squire station wagon onto Highway 5 toward Red Clover. She turns to me, mischief dancing in her eyes. "If there were one thing you could do tonight—and get away with it—what would it be?"

"Anything at all?"

"Anything."

"If I could get away with it—I'd be lying on a blanket at Sadie's Pond with Billy Ray's head resting betwixt my breasts."

Mrs. Harrison giggles. "Woah, little doggie."

"*He ravishes my heart with a glance of his eyes.*"

"Is that Edna St. Vincent Millay?"

"Nope. Song of Solomon. Here's some Edna for you: *My candle burns at both its ends. It will not last the night. But, ah, my foes, and, oh, my friends—it gives a lovely light,* I say with all the drama I can muster.

"Have you talked to your mama about this burning desire of yours?"

"Mama's passionate about many things—but sex isn't one of them."

"You could be wrong. Still water runs deep."

"Daddy being intoxicated so much probably dampened her ardor."

"Well, your ardor could stand to be dampened."

"No ma'am, my ardor should NOT be dampened. The human body is a miracle. I can't imagine anything as delicious as sharing mine with Billy Ray. I believe my body belongs to me, or perhaps I belong to it. I haven't figured out this whole embodiment business."

"Embodiment business? What do you mean?"

"I don't know what I mean. Sometimes I get this feeling that my mind, body, and soul are in perfect harmony. This happens a lot when I'm with Billy Ray. It's not just sexy tingles in our bodies. All these tender feelings pass between us as if our souls are connected. I get the same wonderful feeling when I'm floating in Sadie's Pond, looking up at the clouds. It's that feeling of blisssss," I say, prolonging the word.

"Blisssss?" She mocks me.

"Yes, like every cell in my body is being struck by lightning."

"Well, if you plan to continue your bliss when that young man comes home from the Navy, you might want to consider getting on the pill."

"The idea of disrupting my natural hormones bothers me."

"Sounds like your hormones are disrupting you—same as they did when I was your age," she says, wrinkling her brow. "When a young woman falls in love, her desire builds and builds until she can't help but offer her whole body—because that's what it's made for. But making love is dangerous for a woman, more so than for a man."

"Well, what am I supposed to do? Get myself to a nunnery? Jump off the Great Falls Bridge?"

"Set your sights on something else—like when you focused on spelling and winning the Shirley County Spelldown, instead of worrying about your daddy's drinking all the time. Maybe you could take up horseback riding or write that scholarship application letter to Dr. Oglethorpe at Smith to help sublimate your biological urges."

"Sublimate. Sublimate. Dance to the music!" I sing at the top of my voice, mimicking that crazy song by Three Dog Night about some poor girl sitting on a pillow ready to climb the wall because some boy forgot to invite her to the Celebrity Ball. "Sublimate. Sublimate. Dance to the music!"

Mrs. Harrison laughs like a seven-year-old.

"So you like my Chastity Anthem?"

"You are an absolute nut-ball," she says.

"What I am is a *virgo intacto.*"

"Which is a good thing to be at your age, but before you offer your *sanctum sanctorum* to anyone—please make sure you get on the pill. At the very least, keep condoms with you at all times, and use them. Heck, I'll even buy them for you," she says, her face flushed. "Please talk to your mother—she's not the prude you think she is."

"I've been around that woman going on eighteen years now—you'd think I would have picked up on her wild side by now."

"Talk to her," she says beseechingly, eyes bloodshot.

"What's wrong, Captain? You look tired."

"There's some news I've been keeping from you."

"News, what news?"

"Jack got promoted to the corporate office in New York."

"He's already plant manager of the mill."

"His goal is to be the president of High Industries one day, so director of marketing is the next right step."

"So just like that—you are moving?"

"Yes."

I stare out the window, tears welling in my eyes.

"We can talk about this later when you feel like it," she says apologetically.

"Well, that will be NEVER," I say, reaching for the radio. "Now, if you don't mind, I'd like to listen to some tunes."

"Suit yourself," she says staring at the highway.

I turn the knob to Big Ways and the Flirtations are boo-hoo-hooing about how their lives ain't nothing but heartaches because some man is making them feel uptight. I love the perky beat and strong vocals of Earnestine and Shirley Pearce, two sisters from South Carolina—but their Baby-I'm-Yours attitude irritates the pee out of me. Women need quit singing all those wimpy, love-gone-wrong songs before every drop of romance gets sucked out of the universe like what happened that night at Myrtle Beach with Billy Ray before he left for the Navy.

Strobe lights flash all over the gargantuan dance hall at the Pavilion where hundreds of sweaty teenagers dance to Joni Mitchell's piano music that flows from the speakers like the wild fresh song of an Indian squaw. My hips swivel around and around in an ever widening spiral. I cannot not take my eyes off Billy Ray, his white teeth glowing, hands held high as if he were worshipping everything there ever was or ever will be. Then Joni starts singing in her sparkling voice about a vision she had on the road to Woodstock of bombers turning into butterflies, which made her feel golden as stardust.

But then the DJ announces the last dance, and the most sexy, soulful music explodes into the room. A redheaded-sunburned girl dancing beside me, hollers out Marvin's name. Billy Ray's fingers start snapping—my toes start tapping—and we shake our butts, laughing as if we were dancing on the streets of Motown. And when Marvin Gaye edges his perfect voice into that mighty stream of sound, Billy Ray joins him, singing *Listen baby* to Tammi Terrell, telling her there ain't no mountain high enough—valley low enough—or river wide enough. Then I join in singing the duet with Billy Ray, switching back and forth with Tammi and Marvin, singing about how our love is ALIVE—and it doesn't matter whether we are miles apart—our hands are meant to help each other.

But afterward, we had a kerfuffle that screwed everything up.

I never told anyone about it either. It's a private matter.

Billy Ray has tried to keep the lines of communication open. In his first letter home, he asked polite questions as if we were pen pals. I ripped that letter into pieces, flushed it down the toilet, and replied with a postcard that I would be incommunicado until he heard otherwise. That's when he started sending money to Spencer for albums he thought I might like. Probably thinks it might help tenderize this tough heart of mine. Remembering that night saddens me because our love story pales in comparison to Marvin and Tammi's glorious duet.

CHAPTER 5

New Colossus

I t's after eleven o'clock when Mrs. Harrison drops me off at home. Thank God everyone's asleep—I'm tuckered out from this long, trying day. Trying to impress Dr. Bannister. Trying not to scream when Mrs. Harrison dropped her I might-be-leaving-you-behind bomb. Trying not to be so hard on myself about Billy Ray.

I take a hot bath, which makes me feel like a big old scrambled egg, then go into the kitchen and find a note from Mama saying she and Daddy are leaving for Charleston at six in the morning, and Gloria Jean will pick the twins up after work. Halle-damn-lujah!. Maybe I should follow Mrs. Harrison's advice and write my way out of this red dirt town. I pick up the brochure for the Native Daughter Scholarship on my dresser, turn to the instructions, and read the prompt: *Tell us about a profound educational experience that changed your perception regarding women.* I proceed to address the letter all official like:

Dr. Toby Oglethorpe, Smith College
Northampton, Massachusetts 01063
Re: Native Daughter Leadership Scholarship

Then I practice conscious breathing until my mind clears, and Mrs. Harrison's suggestion pops into my head: "Why not write about when you first heard that Emma Lazarus poem?" So I put myself in a trance, go back to my sixth-grade classroom, and write:

Dear Dr. Oglethorpe:

My most profound educational experience occurred on the first day of sixth-grade, when Mrs. Richards stood beside a poster of the Statue of Liberty and recited "The New Colossus," a sonnet written by Emma Lazarus, whose words convinced me that this Lady of Liberty was different from all others. Her mighty limbs were not made for conquering. The beacon in her hand was no ordinary flame—it was the imprisoned lightning of Mother Nature! Her sculpted lips cried out to me:

> *Give me your tired, your poor,*
> *Your huddled masses yearning to breathe free,*
> *The wretched refuse of your teeming shore.*
> *Send these, the homeless, tempest-tost to me,*
> *I lift my lamp beside the golden door!*

I felt like a big honking bird. I wanted to spread my wings and fly to New York City to find this Colossal Lady of Liberty. I wanted to perch myself on her aquiline nose and listen to her big stony lips whisper, You, my dear, are free. And then it dawned on me that my teacher was a female—the poem was written by a female—and the Statue of Liberty was a gigantic female.

I stop right there, thrilled to the bone, just like in sixth grade. But I'm worn out. No need to finish this letter tonight. My parents are going to Charleston for their anniversary tomorrow, and Gloria Jean's taking the twins off my hands. I'll have some peace and quiet to finish it.

CHAPTER 6

Hot as a firecracker

The next evening, I sit in front of the mirror, envying Gloria Jean's gorgeous red hair as she brushes my shoulder length dark blonde mane, flipping it out real nicely on the ends. "Do you think Mama would notice if I restored my hair to the sun-streaked hair of my youth," I say haughtily.

"Sun-streaked hair of your *youth*? You sound like a Summer Blonde commercial," she says, trying to keep a straight face. "Of course she would notice. She notices everything. Come on, go home with me and the twins. I don't like you staying here alone."

"Absolutely not. Lucinda's coming to spend the night."

"Lucinda's reputation isn't that good, you know?"

"People think she's a floozy just because she's a majorette, but Lucinda appreciates the absurdities of life and she plans to be a pharmacist."

"Baton-twirling pharmacist who appreciates the absurdity of life—sounds like the perfect friend for you."

"Plus she's going to Clemson in the fall—going to be a gen-u-wine Clemson Tiger."

"Come on, help me round up the hellions. I got a bushel of corn to be shucked tonight."

I grab the twins' suitcase, feeling a little envious of Gloria Jean's passion for growing fruits and vegetables. Living in Red Clover suits her, but I have always felt like a monkey dropped into the wrong jungle.

It's dark outside and the twins are running around under the pine trees capturing lightning bugs in mayonnaise jars. I put their suitcase in the trunk. Gloria Jean climbs into her white Grand Prix and toots the horn. The twins run toward the car in a dead heat, yelling Shotgun! Joshua jumps into the front seat and locks the door. Noah climbs into the back seat, muttering jackass.

"Toodle-doo, my little turdlings," I say.

"If we are *your* little turdlings, that means you ain't nothing but a big fat TURD," Josh says, all high and mighty.

Gloria Jean shakes her finger at me. "Girl, you better behave."

"Don't worry about me—I got everything under control."

"See you Friday afternoon," she says and drives away.

LET FREEDOM RING. I prance into my bedroom, take off my shorts and shirt, stretch out on the bed in my bra and panties, and stare at the ceiling. It's almost nine-o'clock and still hot as Hades, but my skin feels like smooth as a baby's against these cool cotton sheets. Last week, I read in an anatomy book that skin is considered an organ. The average adult's weighs seven pounds—and if stretched would cover twenty-five square feet.

When anyone touches my skin as if I really matter—especially Billy Ray—it's better than tasting chocolate, smelling fried chicken, or watching snow fall. I have a deficit in the being touched department. I guess that's why that image of Mama and Daddy laying their hands on me at the same time is emblazoned in my mind. The reason it all came about is because of that first damn bra I wore 24 hours a day like a brace. The metal clasp had caused a terrible rash on my back, so one night, Mama lifted my shirt to show Daddy and he ran his fingers over my skin, which felt a little creepy then. Now, it feels more like a blessing.

I imagine Mama and Daddy in Charleston, riding around in a fancy horse-drawn carriage, munching on hot pecan pralines, their hearts afire. My heart's still afire with longing for Billy Ray—but I am not in the mood for *Lady Chatterley's Lover*. It's loaded with SEX, but has zilch in the ROMANCE department. Tonight, I feel like exploring the luscious fruits in *Song of Solomon*—the most enigmatic seven pages of scripture I've ever read. It's the only book in the Bible that does not even mention God, or the Lord, or the Messiah, or anything of the sort. It's about the divine succulence of human flesh. And the young Shulamite woman is hot as a firecracker, wandering around in the garden of nuts, amongst the juicy pomegranates, tender grapes, and swaying lilies, looking for some good loving.

I grab my white leather Bible from the nightstand, unzip the finicky zipper, turn to Chapter 5 and read the last verse: *His mouth is most sweet: yea, he is altogether lovely. This is my beloved, and this is my friend.* Then I flip back to Chapter 3 and read one of my favorite romantic sentences in the whole Bible: *Saw ye him whom my soul loveth?* It reminds me of poor Juliet hankering out loud: *Wherefore art thou, Romeo?* I flip to Chapter 7 and read another one of my favorites: *I am my beloved's, and his desire is toward me.* I miss everything about Billy Ray—especially his soft luscious lips.

A light breeze blows through my window, lifting the white cotton curtains. Shouts of neighborhood children drift through the air, sounding faint, as if they came from a long time ago. I get that weird betwixt and between feeling that borders on hysteria—like I've been stifling yawns for years and they all want to come out—one at a time in a long series that goes on forever. But if I let the first one out, I will yawn myself to death. To relax, I breathe in all the air I can possibly hold and visualize my lungs fully expanded. Then I exhale through my nose. I continue to breathe deeply until I feel like a white lacy moth floating, floating, floating . . .

I find myself standing ankle deep in the Catawba River, watching the giant egg-yolk of a sun slipping off the horizon. An undertow starts pulling at my feet, gently at first, but it gets more powerful. I look down. The water looks white and foamy. I scoop some into my palm and drink it. It tastes like milk! The river has turned into a raging ocean of milk. I look out at the water. Billy Ray is swimming toward the horizon. He's about twenty feet away, and I holler out his name, but no sound comes out of my mouth. A giant wave swells higher and higher as it hurls toward the shore. I cry out, but again—I have no voice. Billy Ray keeps swimming, unaware of the wave. By the time it gets close to the shore, the white wave is hundreds of feet high. It washes over Billy Ray first—and then me—swallowing us alive.

CHAPTER 7

Sweet Lovin' Son of a Preacher Man

I wake up from my catnap, my mind terribly alert from one of those whopper-sized dreams—the kind my soul dreams up just for me, filled with hidden clues. I can still taste the salty milk on my tongue, but I look at my feet—they sure don't look like they've been standing in an ocean of milk. They look like some poor dirt farmer's. It's half past ten—Lucinda probably won't get here until eleven. Plenty of time to shave my legs and give myself a pedicure so I can avoid her tragedy-of-letting-myself-go lecture.

"Hey Karlene," Lucinda hollers from living room.

I run and unlatch the screen door.

"Come on, let's listen to some music," she says, and I follow as she bugaloos to my room and puts my *Dusty in Memphis* album on the record player. A guitarist plunks out a few riffs, and Dusty's sultry voice sings about Billy Ray, that sweet-lovin' son of a preacher man who *thrilled* her to the bone. You can tell by the emotion in Dusty's voice that she'd give her whole body to that boy if he were around.

Lucinda knows I love this song, even though I say I despise it. She stands in front of the mirror, clutching an imaginary microphone, and croons along with Dusty about Billy Ray stealing kisses from me on the sly and how I'm his girl—and all that baloney. Then she passes the microphone to me, and I wail about how being good is never easy—no matter how hard I try—and that Billy Ray was the only boy who could ever *teach* me anything.

Then Lucinda and I exclaim along with Dusty: *Oh, yes he was,* and bump our butts together like imbeciles until the nerve-wracking song comes to an end. I flop on the bed, but Lucinda shimmy, shimmy, shimmies to my dresser, picks up the tattered paperback of *Lady Chatterley's Lover,* holds it high in the air—and thumps it like Preacher Smoot thumps his Bible.

"Oh no you don't." I try to snatch it from her.

She hugs the book to her chest and bends over so I can't get it. I thrust my hands under her armpits, trying to tickle her, but she clamps her arms tight. I grab a pillow and whop her upside the head, admonishing her, "You ought to be thinking about the Lord, Lucinda Randall!" Then I pummel her again. "God knows—you ought to be thinking about the Lord!"

Lucinda tumbles onto the bed, giggling at my impersonation of Mama. Then she hands me the book. "Read me a bedtime story."

"Are you kidding? This book is a chamber of horrors."

"I don't remember anything horrible."

"What about that morbid scene when Mellors commands Lady Chatterley to lie perfectly still like a corpse, which she does, and he proceeds to ramrod her as if he were the Penetrator and she, his Penetratee?"

"Damn Karlene, you sound like a lawyer using those fancy words," she says fluffing up her pillow. "I have a modeling appointment in Charlotte tomorrow—please go with me," she says in her I'm your best friend, you can't say no voice.

"If you insist."

"Mind turning the light off? I need some beauty sleep," she says, then rolls over and faces the wall.

I turn off the lamp, thinking about how exuberant it felt to belt out "Son of a Preacher Man" with Lucinda. I haven't played it since Billy Ray left for the Navy. Billy Ray is the *grandson* of a preacher man. The first time he stole a kiss from me was in the projection room at Midway Theatre. It thrilled me to the bone, but fifteen minutes later I ended up at the hospital with a serious case of gastritis. Must have worked myself into a frenzy, anticipating that long-awaited kiss.

An image from my dream flashes in my mind of Billy Ray swimming toward a gargantuan wave rising up out of the Ocean of Milk. I'll go to the library in the morning. Maybe Miss Sophia can help me untangle that mysterious milky ocean.

CHAPTER 8

Absurd and Unscriptural

Lucinda drops me off at the library, and I walk up the sidewalk toward Miss Sophia, who's tending her garden out front. She's the one responsible for getting me hooked on Ralph Waldo Emerson back in eighth grade when she recommended *Self Reliance* and *Compensation*, and I gobbled up his philosophy, especially the part about being genuine in all things. That way our actions speak for themselves and we don't have to explain ourselves every second of our lives. Miss Sophia looks up, scissors in one hand, a bouquet of white roses in the other.

"Go on in, honey, you got the place to yourself. I'll be in a minute. Got something for you on those Grimké sisters," she says, her yellowy oniony skin crinkling around her eyes.

"Ever heard of an Ocean of Milk? Had a weird dream about it."

"Might find something in that mythology encyclopedia."

I go inside, pull out the huge green volume, and discover a Hindu myth about how thirteen precious treasures got lost in the Ocean of Milk, including amrita, the *Elixir of Immortality*. So the gods came up with a scheme and enticed the Serpent King and Great Tortoise to churn all the amrita out of the Ocean of Milk, which turned out to be disastrous. But I don't see any connection to my dream about Billy Ray.

Miss Sophia comes in and hands me a folder. "I stayed up half the night reading these letters Sarah Grimké wrote to those Boston preachers, who rebuked the sisters for their audacity to voice their opinion about slavery. She and Angelina were something else. True pioneers. Abolitionists and suffragists."

"I am eager to read the letters and anything else you can find."

"Heard a rumor Mr. Harrison was leaving the mill."

"I'd rather not talk about that topic today."

"Well, I'm here if you want to talk."

"Appreciate your concern," I say, then hurry down the street and into Red Clover Bakery, where Mr. Tobias is boxing up a coconut cake for a blue-haired lady. I plop my book satchel on a table by the window, then walk along the display cases, admiring the fancy cookies, fruit pies with flaky crusts, and chocolate cream pies topped in peaks of golden meringue.

"Reckon you want the usual," Mr. Tobias says, as he puts a cinnamon bun on a plate and pushes it across the counter.

"Reckon I do." I touch the bun to make sure it's hot.

He pours coffee into a beige mug.

"How's that sorry no-count Daddy of yours?"

"Twice the man you'll ever be." I say, tossing out the insult he and Daddy frequently hurl at each other.

I sit at the table, open Miss Sophia's folder, and see the faces of Angelina Grimké and Sarah Grimké staring back at me—stern as can be—as if their frilly bonnets are tied too tight. The article says the Grimké sisters despised the plantation system so much that they moved to Boston and spoke out against slavery, which riled up the clergy. So Sarah wrote a series of scholarly letters to address the ignorant preachers, just like Reverend King did to the clergymen who attacked him over the hullabaloo in Birmingham.

I pick up the first letter, *The Original Equality of Women*. It's dated the 7th month and 11th day of 1837. I do the math—that was 134 years ago. I envision Sarah sitting at a desk in Boston writing this letter, and I feel as if her heart were *beating in my chest*. She addresses the letter *Dear Friend* and starts out boldly, determined to beat those clergymen at their own game. A topnotch scholar, she studied Genesis in the original Greek and Hebrew because she wanted to find out for herself what happened back when *creation swarmed with animated beings that were capable of natural affection*.

Sarah concludes that Genesis did NOT give men power over women and that it was ABSURD and UNSCRIPTURAL to say such a thing. Adam could have rebuked Eve for suggesting they eat forbidden fruit—but he did NOT—which proved he was NOT morally superior. She calls Adam and Eve the *Fallen Pair* which is so poignant I can hardly bear the sound of it.

I sip my coffee and ponder the allegory of the original garden. It occurs to me that if God created *everything*, the serpent could NOT have put itself in the Garden and cannot be blamed. And Eve was terribly curious, but it was God who had created her that way. So Eve cannot be blamed. Adam, on the other hand, was incurious as they come—maybe even a dimwit. God had created *him* that way. Adam cannot be blamed either.

I browse through the folder. Twenty-five letters in all. Each one ends with: *Thine for the oppressed in the bonds of womanhood*. The eloquence makes me want to finish that letter to Dr. Oglethorpe. I pull it from my satchel and read the last paragraph about how I felt like a bird and wanted to fly to New York harbor and see the Statue of Liberty when Mrs. Richards read the "New Colossus" in class. All fired up again, I begin to write.

The whole idea of feminine power must have imprinted itself on me that day. But now, that word "FEMALE" shimmers with even more significance. And just the other day when I rocked in my dead grandma's chair, another word popped into my head. The word was FOREMOTHER. I had never seen the word. I had never heard the word. That's when I had an epiphany, Dr. Oglethorpe: The United States of America lacks a bosom.

I believe America needs to grow a bosom, metaphorically speaking. If women had more say-so in the government of our country, we might not have spent billions of dollars waging a war that has killed 45,000 American soldiers. In Red Clover alone, we have lost seven young men. Not to mention the hundreds of thousands civilian deaths. To change our government's war-mongering policies, women must get elected to the United States Congress. But women are babies at using political power. We did not get the right to vote until 51 years ago. It's time to claim our power. The good news is that women are practical, efficient, resilient, and determined. And on behalf of myself, my mother, and Mrs. Harrison, I will jump through fiery hoops to win this scholarship. I'd like to end my plea with a closing from another native daughter of South Carolina, Sarah Grimké:

Thine for the oppressed in the bonds of womanhood,

Karlene Kaye Bridges

CHAPTER 9

What About Her Future Babies?

At two o'clock sharp, Lucinda and I walk to the registration table in front of the Magnolia Room at the Metroview Hotel behind SouthPark Mall. She's wearing red platform shoes, tight red sweater, and black mini-skirt. The black beret on top of her glossy brown hair adds a French schoolgirl touch to her femme fatale outfit. I stand beside her in my crisp white cotton blouse with cap sleeves, faded bell-bottoms, and my scuffed-up, too-tight red cowboy boots.

"Hello ladies, are you here for the photo shoot?" A young woman says, who looks and sounds just like Miss Georgia from the Miss America Pageant.

"Yes, ma'am. My name is Lucinda Randall."

The woman looks at me. "How about you?"

"Lucinda's the model. I'm just her friend," I say, trying not to stare at the cleavage bulging out of her black V-neck dress.

She looks at me from head to toe.

"Well, you certainly are cute enough."

"She hates the camera," Lucinda says firmly.

"Did you bring your costume and boots?" Miss Georgia says, handing her a clipboard.

"Yes, they're in here." Lucinda holds out her travel bag.

"Good. Go over there and sit beside the other young ladies and fill out the forms. We'll call you when we're ready."

"Thank you," Lucinda says, then pulls me toward a couple of empty chairs and makes me sit beside her.

"What kind of photo shoot is this?"

"They're looking for the sexiest majorette in the Southeast."

"Is it a contest? Do you win a trophy? A car? Cash?"

"Ten thousand dollars."

"Ten thousand dollars! Who in the world would pay ten thousand dollars for a photo of a majorette?"

She leans over and whispers, "Playboy Magazine."

Holy Moly—I can't believe this is happening. I grip her arm. "Come on, leave that stupid clipboard and come with me."

She pulls her arm, resisting.

"Now, Lucinda Randall. Right damn now."

She waves at Miss Georgia. "I'll be right back."

We walk into the fancy restroom with marble floor and gold faucets. Lucinda pulls out a Virginia Slim cigarette, lights it, takes a long puff, and blows smoke out the side of her mouth. I take the cigarette and throw it into the toilet. "You are beautiful enough to be Playmate of the Century, but it's a trap—don't do it."

"That scholarship at Clemson will only cover half of my expenses, and Mama's barely scraping by. I need the money."

"You might as well sew a big old H on your majorette outfit for HUSSY. How will you ever look anyone in the eye?"

"It might be fun to get some attention," she says, fooling with a strand of her hair.

"Attention! You want half the men in America ogling your breasts and derriere? Playboy is a girlie magazine! Thousands of men will be salivating and God knows what else onto your picture for years. Men never throw those magazines away. They hide them under the bed, in the attic, in their closets, and they plaster the centerfolds on the ceilings in their toolsheds like my Uncle Floyd. Once Hugh Hefner gets a load of that body of yours—he'll fly to Red Clover in his fancy jet in his silk pajamas and seduce you to live in his fancy mansion in Chicago with hundreds of other girls in their little bunny cages. It's a trap, I'm telling you, it's a trap."

"Ricky said he thought it was a good idea," she says twirling that strand of hair into a knot.

I light into my Lucinda Randall, you have a brilliant mind, you have to respect yourself sermon, but she about twirls a knot into her hair, probably thinking about Ricky, the former point guard for the Red Clover Tornadoes, who's now the number one salesman at the Chevrolet dealership. Having sex with him must be out of this world.

An acidy burp rises from my stomach sounding like a bullfrog.

Lucinda quits twirling her hair, and I continue my speech. "You are a goddess—a highly intelligent human being. What about your future babies? You want them to see their mama sprawled naked in a halfway pornographic magazine?" I pause for a moment. Step One floats into my head: *Admit you are powerless over every damn thing.* "Okay, Lu, do what you got to do." I stride out of the bathroom and over to the registration table.

"Mind if I take one of these?" I say, picking up a business card for Savoy's Photography in case I decide to investigate this mess further.

"Take as many as you like," Miss Georgia says.

I thank her and walk to the elevator.

Lucinda comes over, looks at me with tormented eyes.

"Karlene, come on, go to the photo session with me."

"Go to the mall with me," I say in my demanding voice.

She just stands there looking helpless. There has to be some way to get her out of here without dragging her. I glance at the four young women waiting for their photo opportunity. "You're going to have to wait at least a couple hours before your session. Come on—shop with me. You can come back in an hour."

The elevator door opens. "Come on, Lu, please."

She looks down at her platform shoes. I stride into the elevator, push the lobby button, and the door closes.

I close my eyes and breathe deeply, trying to detach from the situation—but an image of Lucinda wearing pink bunny ears appears in my mind—but it's immediately replaced by the Grimké Sisters in their tight frilly bonnets, just shaking their heads.

CHAPTER 10

Light My Fire

SouthPark Mall is crowded with shoppers, many of them dressed in Levi's or Bermuda shorts, but over at the Record Bar, there's a bunch of hippie types, a la John and Yoko wandering around in faded jeans and tie dyed shirts. A gigantic poster with a naked-from-the-waist-up photo of Jim Morrison hangs in the window display. Scripted underneath in bold letters:

James Douglas Morrison
December 8, 1943—July 3, 1971

A vision of Jim flashes in my mind from The Ed Sullivan show. He's dressed in tight black pants, black leather jacket, and white shirt—holding the microphone close to his lips with both hands, eyes closed. His curly hair looks fresh and clean. His demeanor is almost bashful. He starts off singing namby-pambyish to some girl, but then gets totally direct about the fact that together, they could get much higher.

You cannot really tell what kind of high he's talking about. Probably not the gee-whiz, I'm-in-love-with-you kind of high—more likely the high that comes from taking LSD or peyote or psilocybin mushrooms. The song has a deep watery undertow feeling to it—except for when Jim shouts *Fire* in that gravelly voice of his. My favorite line is about not wallowing in the MIRE, which rhymes with all those other long "I" words: LIAR, FIRE, HIGHER, and funeral PYRE. I've always had a doomy feeling about Jim's band. That name of theirs conjures up all the heavy metaphorical doors in our lives—and where they might lead. I can't imagine how Jim's girlfriend felt when she found him in his apartment in Paris—his light snuffed out for all eternity.

I stroll toward the Intimate Bookshop that's crammed with hundreds of people and thousands of new books. The Intimate is not reverent like the library—it's like a gourmet store for the mind. When I first started shopping here, I used to flit around from one department to another like a drunken butterfly. Nowadays, I hang out in the fiction, poetry, and psychology areas. Featured in the window display are *The Sensuous Man, Future Shock* and *The Female Eunuch,* which has a surrealistic painting on the cover of the disembodied naked torso of a woman hanging from a curtain rod. The breasts, pelvis, and mound of Venus are anatomically correct—but a handle protrudes from the sides of both hips, which makes me shudder at the implications.

It's no fun shopping without Lucinda. The mall opened last February. Lucinda talked me into skipping class that day. And when I first saw this humongous concrete building rising out of what used to be a cow pasture, I thought it was a huge penitentiary. Looking at the behemoth structure gave me an eerie feeling, as if a whole other kind of world had been born.

I look over at the Orange Julius stand and realize I'm thirsty. No customers standing in line. Gayle, the cute freckle-faced girl behind the counter recognizes me and waves. I walk up to her, say hello, and order a large Julius. She asks where Lucinda is. I tell her about the modeling appointment, leaving out the naked part. She asks if I want the raw egg option, and I tell her I prefer my eggs scrambled. She grins as she prepares my creamy orange drink, then hands it to me—

nice and frothy. A handsome businessman strides up to the counter like he owns the mall, so I say adios.

I don't feel like shopping, so I stroll past Morrison's Cafeteria into the parking lot and make my way to SouthPark Cinema. According to the marquee, my choices are *Willy Wonka and the Chocolate Factory* and *Carnal Knowledge.* The Willy Wonka poster is simple—with a white background. Willy stands there, arms spread wide, juggling the letters of a delicious-sounding word: *Scrumdiddlyumptious. Carnal Knowledge* has a stark white poster with no pictures, just the actors' names in bold black type and the title underneath in bold RED letters:

> *Mike Nichols, Jack Nicholson,*
> *Candice Bergen, Arthur Garfunkel,*
> *Ann-Margret, and Jules Feiffer.*
> *Carnal Knowledge.*

The poster doesn't match up with the racy title. Guess I need to find out for myself. I walk to the ticket booth and ask the cute, pimply-faced boy for a ticket. He snickers when he hands it to me, eyes averted. I bypass the refreshment stand and walk past a half dozen other loners before taking an aisle seat seven rows from the front. My boots are killing me. I pull them off and sit cross-legged, rubbing my swollen feet. The movie opens with two college roommates lying on their beds in their dorm room late at night, talking about how much they like to feel girls up. But if the girl lets them feel her up—they confess they don't like her anymore.

Right away I realize any girl who loves those two college boys is doomed, and pretty soon, I realize that Jonathan, played by Jack Nicholson, is a liar and manipulator—so I nickname him Snake. Art Garfunkel's character is gawky and flighty, so I call him Canary.

Canary falls in love with a classy blonde coed and proceeds to have sex with her pronto. Snake finds out and seduces her too. They're both screwing her—but Canary doesn't have a clue.

After college, Canary becomes a physician and marries the blonde, who becomes a housewife and totally disappears from the movie. Snake becomes a highfalutin lawyer and has sex with one woman after another, but abandons each one when he discovers her breasts aren't large enough—legs aren't shapely enough—or bottom isn't curvy enough.

Years roll by while Snake continues to search for Miss Perfect in Every Aspect. Then one night his wandering eyes zero in on the cleavage of the Ann-Margret character named Bobbie, who looks as if she's had sex a million times. And before you can say lickety-split, they're shacked up, and Bobbie's drinking liquor and stuffing her face with bonbons, too despondent to get out of bed. One morning, Snake is running around the bedroom in tight white jockey shorts, getting dressed for work—when out of the blue, Bobbie says she wants to get married. Jonathan lights in on her, calling her *a ball-busting, castrating, son of a cunt bitch.*

I can't bear that foul-mouthed creep—or Bobby mewing like a dying kitten. I force my swollen feet into my too-tight boots and leave the theater, wondering what imbecile called this movie a bittersweet comedy. The way these two dimwits center the entire universe around their penises is a goddamn tragedy.

I put on my tight boots and hobble outside toward the Metroview Hotel. Lucinda's walking toward me, her head down. She used to have more sparkle than anyone I ever met—until her daddy fell in love with Darla at the Red Clover Telephone Company—and left his family last Christmas. That's when she started modeling, to pay for her own keep, so to speak. She's a model for Belk Department Store advertisements that always look spectacular. But this Playboy bunny business gives me the same wormy feeling I had about Bobbie in the movie—that the best days of Lucinda's life might have already been lived.

But then I realize Lucinda has her own life to live, and so do I.

I pray to God I will *not* be like Susan in that godforsaken movie screwing around with two creepy guys. And I pray Lucinda will *not* be like Bobbie begging some dumbass lawyer to marry her. But an image of that weary sex kitten on the cover of *Life* flashes in my mind. If poor Ann-Margret got messed up by *just pretending* to be Bobbie—I hate to imagine how Lucinda will feel after a million eyeballs inspect her naked body up close and personal.

CHAPTER 11

Bowl of Red Pears

Lucinda's stretched out on the reclined bucket seat, sleeping or pretending to sleep while I steer her Mustang south on Highway 200 toward home. I saw my first ghost with Lucinda. Canned my first jar of peaches. Learned how to suck my cheeks in to make my face look slim. Just looking at her, knowing she'll be leaving for college soon, makes me appreciate that old cliché, sight for sore eyes.

Dionne Warwick's singing that internal monologue song on the radio, practicing what she wants to say to some guy she's known for awhile. How she wants him—and loves him—and needs him—and all that baloney—but she does not have the guts to tell him. I admire Dionne's radiant smile with those crooked teeth of hers. I just wish she'd sing a song with some meat on its bones like Aretha.

Lucinda sits up. "How long I been sleeping?"

"We're almost home. I need to drop by the Harrisons'."

"You haven't been babysitting lately, what's up?"

"James is at baseball camp and Celia is staying with her grandma for two weeks."

"Those two are the happiest kids I ever met."

"You'd be happy, too, if you lived in a house that had wall-to-wall carpet, four bedrooms, and an intercom system. And that library of theirs—I'd cut off one of my ears for that."

"You're lucky to have someone like Mrs. Harrison in your life. I never had a teacher show that kind of interest in me."

"She's trying to brainwash me to take that Native Daughter scholarship at Smith College if they offer it."

"Worse things to be brainwashed about," she says, which makes me feel like a selfish brat.

When we get to the fancy entrance to Catawba Hills, I turn onto Sherwood Forest Drive. We pass the sprawling contemporary of Mr. Broadwater, the editor of the *Red Clover Chronicle*. He's standing on the front porch playing pocket pool as usual. "What that man needs is some good, good loving," Lucinda says in her fake purring voice.

"When he gets his hairy-knuckled hands on your naked pictorial, he'll get relief for the rest of his life."

"Nothing wrong with getting some *relief*—you ought to try it sometime."

I ignore her snide comment, then turn into the Harrisons' driveway and park behind a brand new baby blue Thunderbird convertible.

"Come on Lu, go inside with me."

She scoots into the driver's seat. "Be back in half an hour."

I jog through the back gate, my nose twitching at the smell of rosemary and thyme. Mrs. Harrison is reading on the back porch. She gets up and unlatches the screen door. "Hey, Jelly Bean."

"Whose Thunderbird is that out front?"

"Jack bought it," she says hurriedly. "Come in, I bought some of those pears you like."

I sit across the table from her and admire the dark red pears brimming out of a white ceramic bowl. I take one and hold it in the palm of my hand. "You know something, Captain Mathilda? If I had never met *you*, I would never have tasted one of these scrumptious pears, and if you had not taken me to the Carolina Theater in Charlotte, I might never have seen Julie Andrews whirl around on the top of the mountain, lift her arms and sing—"

She belts out: *The hills are alive with the sound of music—with songs they have sung for a thousand years*, but when she sees my lips in full pouting mode, she quits singing.

"Thanks Madam, may I finish my soliloquy?"

"By all means, proceed."

"If I had never met you—I would have never heard your *Making Out With Boys Speech*. The one about how our eyes are our most important sex organ—and that before I ever let a fellow unzip his pants in my presence—I should stare deep into his eyes until I see the truth in them. "

"Yikes! I don't remember saying that."

"Well, you certainly did. You talked about how Jack had stormed into your life—and before you knew it—you were living in a fancy house, with two kids and a husband. And you also had a full-time teaching job. You said being Mrs. Jack Harrison felt like a *sacrificium intellectus*—a sacrificing of your intellect. And that you had always wanted to do something great like paint a masterpiece or be an actress. And you encouraged me to remain a *virgo intacto* as long as possible."

"I talk too much," she says, as if she's ashamed of herself.

"Best conversation I ever had. Wrote down every word."

"I'd love to get my hands on that speech," she says, squeezing my hand. "When my little Celia turns fourteen—I'll give it to her—just like I gave it to you."

I pull off my boots. "These dogs of mine are killing me."

"You left your tennis shoes in the den by the sofa."

"Hot diggedy dog." I stroll into the den, my fingers gliding across the spines of leather-bound copies of Hemingway, Emily Dickinson, Ralph Waldo Emerson, and Mark Twain. I sit on the sofa and slip my aching feet into my roomy Converse basketball shoes.

"Made some toffee," Mrs. Harrison says, handing me a plate wrapped in foil, and we go outside.

The Mustang pulls into the driveway, and the future playmate gets out. I wished I had discussed the naked picture fiasco with Mrs. Harrison, but I don't think she has the highest opinion of Lucinda.

"Hey Mrs. Harrison," Lucinda says, running her fingers across the white ragtop of the new baby blue Thunderbird. "Got yourself a beauty here."

"It's a bribe from my husband. He said we could move to Connecticut instead of New York—and that I deserved a new car."

"You're moving?" Lucinda says, startled.

"Yes," Mrs. Harrison says, surprised she doesn't know.

"How soon?" Lucinda says.

"Just found out today—right after Halloween."

My bottom lip trembles like a baby's.

I grab the plate of toffee and stride to the Mustang. Lucinda runs ahead of me and opens the passenger door. I slump into the bucket seat. Mrs. Harrison squats by my door.

"Great to see you, Mrs. Harrison," Lucinda says.

"Ditto," I say, feeling numb as a basketball.

"How about spending the night, Jelly Bean?"

"Not tonight," I say staring through the windshield.

As Lucinda drives away, the cicadas screech as if they're out to devour the world.

CHAPTER 12

Origin of the Milky Way

When we get to my house, it's completely dark. I turn on the porch light, and Lucinda sits on the porch swing. I go to the kitchen and remove the aluminum foil from Mrs. Harrison's plate. A bolt of sorrow zaps my heart when I see those little squares of toffee with almond bits sprinkled on top. Mrs. Harrison's toffee is the most scrumptious candy I have ever tasted— but I can't bear to eat a single piece tonight. I cover the plate and take two glasses of iced tea outside.

Lucinda has taken off her sexy platform shoes, her long legs stretched out in front of her. The porch light is harsh, casting yellow daggers into the darkness. I hand her a glass of tea and sit down beside her. She pushes off with her foot, rocking us gently. We swing a while, sipping tea, thinking our own thoughts.

"How do you feel about Mrs. H. leaving?"

"Like a big rusty screw has been screwed into my heart."

"How did you become so close?"

"In eighth grade, she strutted into my Latin class dressed in a white toga, saying she was an extraordinary individual, who fully intended to transform each and every one of us knuckleheads into a Latin scholar by the end of the year—no matter how much suffering it caused. Then she asked us to introduce ourselves and tell her something important about ourselves. When I said I planned to win the Shirley County Spelldown, she offered to be my spelling coach. Her personality enthralled me so much that I told her if she ever needed a babysitter, I was the absolute best. A week later, I met the whole family, and everything just clicked. The best word to describe the Harrisons is gen-u-wine."

"No one has ever called me ge-u-wine," Lucinda says in that gravelly, premenstrual voice of hers.

"Lucinda Randall, you are beyond genuine. You are fetching, captivating, and drop dead—"

"Gorgeous," she spits out the word distastefully. "Promise you won't ever describe me with that stupid cliché again."

"I promise. Come on, let's go look at the stars."

I pull her into the yard and find a spot away from the glare of the streetlight. We lie in the grass right beside each other. And as I look up at the billions of stars spiraling in the black velvety sky, I get this feeling as if I am God Almighty, high above, looking through a giant telescope. And what I see are two big-hearted, high-spirited girls stretched out in the front yard of a small, white, wooden house in the town of Red Clover, located in the bottom-of-the-totem-pole state of South Carolina, in the God-blessed United States of America, situated on the continent of North America, on Planet Earth—which for some damn reason—is the only planet *not* named after a god. Seeing our situation so clearly from so far away gives me the heebie-jeebies—so I force myself back into my body lying on the scorched grass beside my best girlfriend.

"Hey, Lu, you ever heard the myth about how the Milky Way was created?"

"Nope."

"One fine morning, Hera wakes up and finds a baby boy suckling her breast. Then she looks at Zeus the Philanderer, sleeping beside her, and realizes he has sneaked another one of his mortal bastards into her bed to drink her immortal milk. She snatches that baby away from her breast—and voila! Milk spurts from her nipple and spirals into the Milky Way."

"Good Lord, I will *never* be able to look up at the sky at night without seeing milk swirling out of Hera's breasts."

I want to say: *It's hard to look at you without thinking of your body splashed across Playboy magazine for the whole horny world to see,* but I have no right to judge her.

"Hey, Lu. It's a beautiful night—let's go to Sadie's Pond."

A car horn blares and Ricky Worth's black Impala skids to a stop in front of the house. He and Spencer get out and walk over to us. "What's up, pussycats?" Ricky says.

"We're going to Sadie's Pond—want to go?" Lucinda says.

"Can't think of anywhere else I'd rather be," Ricky says.

"Come on, let's change our clothes," Lucinda says.

We go into my room and I slip out of my best jeans and slide into raggedy cutoffs. Lucinda shimmies out of her *femme fatale* outfit into a pair of skin-tight, hip-hugging bell-bottoms and a skimpy t-shirt that shows off the bounciest breasts in Shirley County.

"Come on girl, shake a tail feather. There's a couple of boys outside, waiting to be bewildered," she says and saunters outside.

I go into the bathroom and squirt Crest onto my toothbrush. The girl in the mirror brushes her teeth furiously and gazes at me with stormy blue eyes, curious as to what kind of girl I aim to be: the *boy-bewildering* kind—or the *boy-befriending* kind I have always been.

CHAPTER 13

Runaway train

We fly down Hwy. 903 in Ricky's white Impala, on loan from the Red Clover Motor Company, where he works in the summer. Lucinda's head rests on his shoulder. Spencer sits beside me in the back seat, our thighs barely touching, which makes me feel like a caution light at a busy intersection, blinking yellow-dark, yellow-dark, yellow-dark. Up ahead, I see the crooked steeple of the country church rising above the scrubby pines. "Turn right!"

Ricky turns and drives down the dusty road until we come to a clearing and he parks in front of a cute stone cottage surrounded by hydrangea bushes with blossoms as big as my head. The front door and windows have been boarded up for years.

"This place is amazing," Spencer says.

"My great aunt Sadie lugged half the rocks to build it."

"Let's build a bonfire," Spencer says, then takes my hand. "We'll go this way, gather some firewood, and meet you on the other side of the pond."

After a few steps down the path, I pull my hand away from Spencer's and take off running, kicking my legs high like a long-legged African in the Olympics. Spencer runs past me, then turns around, and starts running backward. He's ten feet away, pacing himself with my stride. I scramble past him and sprint as fast as I can—my heart pumping like one of those cartoon hearts beating outside of my chest. I look over my shoulder. Spencer is running toward me at half-throttle, as if he has all the time in the world.

I turn around and start running backward. He takes off his shirt and flings it into the air, belting out *Hi de ho, hi de hi—gonna get me a piece of the sky* in his deep manly voice, as if his tongue made up the song on the spot. I take long deep breaths until highly oxygenated blood floods my brain, putting me in an alert, dreamlike state. When he gets within five feet, Spencer slows down and stops. So do I. We stand there, face-to-face, three feet apart, galvanized, as if we're standing at the edge of the world. He takes a step, then another. His face is so well lit by the almost full moon, I can see the stubble on his face. I allow his lips to touch mine once—twice, but then I force myself to pull away. "Hey, we can't make a fire without any wood."

By midnight, the bonfire has burned down into a snap, crackle, and pop campfire. Lucinda and Ricky are curled up together under the flimsy quilts. Ricky's sweet-talking her and she's cooing like a turtledove. Spencer has paddled Aunt Sadie's old wooden canoe out to the middle of the pond. I'm sitting up front on the bottom hugging my knees to my chest. He's in the back, wailing away on his harmonica. Some notes skip over the pond like smooth stones—others float away on the cool breeze. He quits playing and sings in a hoarse bluesy voice about how the sky is crying and tears are rolling down the street—and how he's trying to find his baby and wonders where she can be. Then he walks to the crossbar on his knees and crooks his finger for me to come to him.

The haughty *virgo intacto* inside me says it's time to paddle back to shore before I get into trouble. But my skin aches to be touched. I scoot forward on my knees until Spencer and I are a few inches apart. My face tilts up to his. He traces my lips with the tip of his finger, and lets it rest there. My lips, of their own accord, suck it every so gently, which makes me feel like a firecracker a second away from *kaboom*. I force myself to pull away, then stand and dive into the water, feeling like a crazy catfish of a girl.

Later, on the drive home, Lucinda and Ricky are in the back seat, nodding off from drinking too much Boone's Farm strawberry wine. I'm sitting up front with Spencer, waving my arm back and forth against the wind, as that mournful singer hollers out the last *No—no-no-no-no-no-no!* at the end of "The Night they Drove old Dixie Down."

"How could anyone write a song so devastating?" I say.

"Death wrote that song," Spencer says, his profile carved in stone. "When that Confederate soldier starts humming in that sad tone and introduces himself as Virgil Caine and talks about the horrors of the war back in the winter of '65, you know Old Virgil is a ghost and he's mourning his dead brother and the buddies he lost in the war, but Virgil's also remembering the sweetness of his life with his wife back in Tennessee before the war," he says glancing sideways.

"That part really got to me, it's understated, but powerful."

"Before my daddy went to Korea, Mama said he was high-spirited and dependable, but he came back reckless and somber. Now, he's shacking up with a girl named Darla, who's just a few years older than me."

He has never brought up the Darla scandal before, so I keep quiet.

"Since I got my draft letter, I've been trying to write a song about the different kinds of roads a person can take in life—like the *Devil's Crossroads* where you sell your soul to Satan like Robert Johnson did down in Mississippi. Maybe that's what my daddy did when he first laid eyes on Darla."

"I wouldn't know," I say, perplexed by the concept of soul-selling.

"Want to hear a couple of verses of my song?"

"Yes, my dear sir."

Spencer sings in a lilting baritone voice:

> *Don't you think it's time to take the high road*
> *cause you been down all the others—*
> *the dead ends and the yellow brick*
> *and the long and winding ones?*
>
> *You been to the devil's crossroad*
> *five hundred times*
> *and every time you go there*
> *you lose your money or your mind.*

"Thought-provoking lyrics with a cool country vibe," I say, amazed he's able to write such a gutsy song with Uncle Sam yanking his strings.

"Glad you like it."

We ride for a while in silence. I want to tell him his sister Lucinda might have ventured onto the Highway to Hell with that naked picture-taking session she had today. I glance back at the drunken lovebirds, who are fast asleep, and a new line to Spencer's song pops into my head: *On the Road to Hell you don't find no Highway Patrol.*

"How do you feel about the Harrisons leaving?" he says.

"Like *Nowhere Girl* sitting in *Nowhere Land*, making all my *nowhere plans* for nobody."

"Well, Nowhere Girl, your life might be a mess—but it is very *well expressed.*" His face breaks into a grin.

I can't believe I'm sitting here beside such a talented, clever young man. What is going to happen to him? Will he be killed in a godforsaken jungle? Or be forced to drop bombs on innocent civilians? Step One comes to mind: *Admit you are powerless over every damn thing.* And I realize I am powerless over Spencer's fate. And then I think about how abruptly I left Mrs. Harrison today after she said they were moving earlier than expected. I am powerless over her. She has her own life to live and her own sorrows to deal with. To turn down her offer to spend the night was idiotic.

When we get near the entrance to Catawba Hills, I ask Spencer to take me to the Harrisons'. My wish is his command, and he turns the Impala into the circular driveway and parks behind Mr. Harrison's Cadillac. "See you tomorrow?"

"I've got a lot on my plate, but thanks for bringing me here."

"Goodbye Nowhere girl," he says, then zooms away.

In the backyard, the Harrisons are smooching like teenagers in the fancy hammock that hangs between two huge oak trees. I stride over to them and put my hands on my hips like I'm the love police. "What's going on here?"

Mrs. Harrison grins. "Just enjoying ourselves."

"Our last night without the kids." Mr. Harrison says, winking. "Nana brings them home tomorrow."

"If it's okay, I'd like to accept your offer to spend the night."

"Sure," Mrs. Harrison says. "I put a book on your bed. The author's feisty—thought she might inspire you to write that letter to Smith College."

"I got a good start already, but I could use a little inspiration."

I walk through the spotless kitchen into the den, thinking about the disturbing things I encountered today. Young girls waiting in line to have naked pictures taken of themselves. People saying the

"F" word in a movie and screwing each other hard-heartedly. Me sucking Spencer's finger and jumping into Sadie's Pond like a stupid girl.

But I could not help myself.

The urge was beyond my control.

Mrs. Harrison is right. Sex is a runaway train.

I descend the stairs, feeling ten years older. But then as I pass Celia and James' rooms with their names on the door and then see *my* name on the door of *my* room, I feel like the luckiest girl in Shirley County.

I plop onto my bed and pick up the book Mrs. Harrison left for me. It has a scarlet cover with *How Never to Be Tired* written in bold gold letters. The author's signature, Marie Beynon Ray, is written in gold too. I open it and read the title page: *How Never to Be Tired* or *Two Lifetimes in One*. Odd as hell to put "or" between the two titles—as if they're asking the reader to choose the title they like best.

But I am too damn tired to think tonight, much less read.

I turn off the lamp and fashion a prayer straight from my heart: *Dear Holy Spirit of Mary, please help Spencer Randall. He's a good man with a terrible problem of being drafted. I'm terribly attracted to him, as you know, and growing very fond of him. Please lead us both in the direction we should go. Help me decide what to do about Lucinda's naked picture situation. Bless the Harrisons as they prepare to move. And bless Billy Ray the Handsome Sailor Man, wherever he is.*

CHAPTER 14

Purple Haze

Friday afternoon, I'm sitting on the front porch swing waiting for Gloria Jean to bring the twins home, reading *How Never to Be Tired*. Marie Beynon Ray is one of the perkiest, most inspiring authors I have ever encountered. She's all jazzed about the Human Dynamo and what she calls the "principles of tirelessness." The main point she's trying to convey is that BEING TIRED IS NOT NORMAL—which is perfectly exemplified in Noah and Joshua and most of the children in the world—they rarely get tired.

Chapter One, is titled "Energy to Burn." And it's about Rodin, the sculptor, and other famous men, such as Napoleon, Carnegie, Rockefeller, and Alexander Graham Bell. The author claims these people were giants of energy. And she's rhapsodic about a Spanish matador named Cagancho whom she saw kill seven bulls in one afternoon, but killing a perfectly decent bull sounds like murder to me.

Her book is hunky-dory so far—except she hasn't included any women as giants of energy like Lucille Ball or Carol Burnett or Marie Curie or Helen Keller or Mamie Eisenhower or the Grimké sisters. It's sort of implied that the author herself is a giant of energy.

Gloria Jean blows the horn as the Grand Prix skids to a stop in the driveway. She drags herself out of the car and stands there with a half-crazed look on her face, her red hair pulled into a ponytail. "For God's sake, please help me with these pollywogs. I totally forgot what a handful they can be."

Joshua tumbles onto the gravel driveway, pushed by Noah, who bounds out of the car and stands over him like a Roman Centurion. I rush out to stop the murderous charade. "Listen, you creeps, if I see you put one finger on each other, I will duct tape your mouths and throw you into the crawl space. Go play in the back yard."

They take off running. Gloria Jean plops down on the porch swing, crossing her eyes in exasperation. "Noah has gone straight from being a wimp to being a bully."

"I told you he's a mercurial child."

"Mercurial? What does that mean?"

"Prone to feistiness and mood swings."

"Spencer asked me to give this to you" she says, handing me a bag from Flower Power.

I reach into the bag and pull out the new album by Stephen Stills. The cover has a whimsical feel. Stephen sits on a bench with snow-covered trees in the background, playing his guitar. A fake baby giraffe stands beside him as if entranced by the music. Spencer knows I love Crosby, Stills, Nash, and Young, but I did NOT order this record. And I did NOT answer the phone that's been ringing off the hook. Thought it might be Spencer calling the Makeout Queen of Shirley County, and I had nothing to say.

Daddy whirls his red Fairlane into the driveway and lays down on the horn. Mama gets out, wearing her black slacks, red blouse and expensive red leather sandals she bought on sale at Belk Department Store. Daddy walks around to the trunk, grabs my scratched-up red Samsonite, and they walk to the porch. "Where are the boys?" Mama says.

"Playing in the back yard," I say.

Gloria Jean latches onto Mama as if Mama had been on a World Tour instead of a two-night trip to Charleston. Daddy looks at me, a flash of worry in his eyes. I shrug my shoulders. Finally, she releases Mama and motions her and Daddy to the swing. Then Gloria Jean just stands there, swaying from side to side, as if she's shy about something.

Finally, she blurts out, "I just left Doc Smith's office."

Mama looks Gloria Jean up and down, "Anything wrong?"

"No, nothing's wrong, but I might be having twins."

"Twins, good Lord," Mama says, then jumps up and hugs Gloria Jean. Daddy walks over, wraps his arms around both of them, giving them a big old manly squeeze.

I leave their little love triangle, go inside, and put on a pot of coffee, wondering why she didn't mention the superfluous baby to me. Probably the same reason I didn't mention my make-out session with Spencer last night—we're just not as close as we used to be.

I turn on the radio. Jimi Hendrix is tearing up his upside-down psychedelic guitar, playing those heart-stabbing notes, and as the drummer starts pounding, I grab two wooden spoons and bang them on the swirly green Formica tabletop, wailing along with Jimi about how we cannot continue to go like this—with purple haze in our eyes—so we just excuse ourselves and kiss the sky.

Banging the spoons lifts my spirits, but an image of poor Jimi choking on his own vomit comes into my head so I put the spoons away. The coffee's through percolating, so I pour myself a cup and take a long slurp. I look out the window. Daddy's playing catch with Joshua and Noah leans against the poplar tree, waiting for his turn.

Mama and Gloria Jean mosey around in the garden, talking about whatever it is they talk about when I'm not around. *Wendell this. Wendell that. Daddy this. Daddy that. Babies this. Babies that.* I must have turned into a damn misanthrope overnight. This baby business leaves me cold. Most mothers are starved for freedom, whether they realize it or not. Babies are nothing but work, work, and more work. Twins are nothing but TORTURE.

Gloria Jean has a demanding job at Catawba Insurance Company and a two-acre garden and a house to care for. She also sells Tupperware, to help save money for the baby. An image of Gloria Jean with her tiny waist, dressed in her blue satin prom dress comes into my head. Twins. Good Lord. She's way too tiny to carry two babies.

Mama comes in the back door and we chitchat about the beautiful gardens they saw at Magnolia Plantation. I hand her the new issue of *Better Homes and Gardens* and tell her I'm fixing fantail shrimp and French fries for supper tonight, to go sit on the sofa, and I'll bring her a cup of coffee.

"What's this Queen of Sheba treatment?" she says and smiles.

"It's not every day a woman finds out she's having multiple grandbabies."

"And it's not every day a girl finds out she's going to have twin nephews or nieces—so *you* won't be cooking dinner. Your daddy is going to the fish camp to buy our supper in a few minutes, but I sure would like a cup of coffee," she says, then traipses out of the kitchen.

Having daddy to herself for a couple of days must have put that sparkle in her eyes. Or maybe it's twin grandbabies. I pour her a cup of coffee and take it outside. She's talking all friendly to someone on the phone about coming to the AA shindig tomorrow at High Mills Park.

She turns her back and whispers, "It's Karlene" to whomever she's talking to, and hangs up.

"Who was that?"

"None of your business," she says lightheartedly.

I walk outside, happy to get out of the kitchen. A cool breeze wafts across my skin, whooshing me right out of Red Clover. I find myself in New York City, wearing a gauzy purple dress, strolling along in Central Park. Elegant sandals cover my slender, pedicured feet. Out on the lawn, a lover awaits. I can't see his face. Maybe it's Billy Ray—or Spencer—or some entirely new DREAMBOAT. He's sitting on a blanket, strumming a guitar, counting the times he'll get to kiss me. I pull a half-sucked Tootsie Roll Pop from my pocket, stick it in my mouth, and bite down hard. My teeth pierce the cherry-flavored exterior. The dark taste of chocolate explodes on my tongue.

Later that night, I'm sweating like a piglet, staring at the cover of my Stephen Stills album. Wish I were Stephen sitting on that bench, strumming my guitar with that red polka dot giraffe standing beside me ankle deep in the snow. If this were my album, I would have titled it, *Plight of the Snow Giraffe*, but the eponymous title is perfect since Stephen is trying to distinguish himself as a solo artist—separate from Crosby, Nash, and Young.

It was kind of Spencer to give me the record. I called to thank him while ago, but got no answer, which is probably a good thing. I put the record on the stereo and lie perfectly still on the cotton sheets. It's so hot I can barely breathe.

The music starts out hot and spicy—guitars strumming—organist pounding out shrill, razor edged notes. It's that hit song that encourages anyone who's lonely and confused to get it together with the person they happen to be with—rather than waiting for their so-called baby who's so far away.

The song's message is perfectly clear: *Love the one you're with. Love the one you're with.* Once that pounding music and suggestive lyrics start swirling inside some lonely girl—she's liable to do almost anything. I appreciate Spencer giving me the record—but I need to starve the little seed of lust that's been planted between us before it sprouts into a giant beanstalk of desire. Tonight, I'm going to love the one I'm with: ME, MYSELF, and I.

I turn off the stereo and walk to the wooden shelf Billy Ray built to keep the snow globes he'd given me. I pick up the first one—it's corny as they come—a snowman in a black top hat holds the hand of a snow-woman sporting a red beret. Billy Ray gave it to me to celebrate the most spectacular touchdown I ever made. I shake the globe, and the snow swirls me back into a Technicolor movie of that afternoon.

Billy Ray and I are in Lucinda and Spencer's front yard, playing football in the snow. We're on opposite teams. Spencer is quarterbacking my team and flirting with me like crazy. Billy Ray has sacked Spencer at least six times, and he's quarterbacked his team to a 12-0 lead. I am determined to score, but it's hard to see the football with so much snow swirling around us.

Finally, I see an opening and sprint as fast as I can toward the goal. Spencer sees me and throws a high arcing pass. I jump into the air, catch it, and make a dash toward the green garden hose used to mark the goal line. The moment I cross it, someone grabs me around my calves and pulls me down. Snow fills my nostrils. I look back and see it's Billy Ray who tackled me. I flip myself over and rub snow into his face. Then suddenly, he's sitting on top of me, his eyes blazing like sparklers. I stare back at him, entranced. The snow flutters around us as if we were captured in a glittery crystal globe all by ourselves. My body feels electrified, as if it could light up the whole world.

The snow has settled on the ground around the cute couple. I put down the globe and pick up the second one that has a little Amish boy and Amish girl holding hands. I shake it gently and mesmerize myself back to that delicious moment with Billy Ray sitting on top of me, our eyes locked, and he says, "You look amazing."

Suddenly, we're surrounded. The others hurl snowballs at us.

"No humping eighth-graders in my front yard," Spencer says.

Billy Ray tackles Spencer, pushes his face in the snow, and says, "I'm not humping anybody." He helps me up, congratulates me on my touchdown, and then starts apologizing. I tell him not to worry—that we were just playing football. I say goodbye to Lucinda and give Spencer and the rest of the dumbasses the evil eye.

I look down at the globe in my hand. The snow has settled onto the ground around the poor, straight-laced Amish couple—who look as if they never had a sexy moment in their entire lives.

PART II

Dreamboat

Love and do what you will.

— St. Augustine

CHAPTER 15

Oh Happy Day

At eight-thirty the next morning, I wake up to another scorcher. Not a hint of a breeze. I go to the kitchen to help Mama with the cooking for the picnic. Hell's bells. She's already fried two chickens, made a huge bowl of potato salad, deviled two dozen eggs, brewed a fresh gallon of tea, and baked two of her famous lemon meringue pies. There's some coffee left in the percolator, so I pour myself a cup and walk to the back door. Mama is out in the garden, gathering tomatoes. She deserves a good breakfast this morning—and some peace and quiet—I'll let the twins sleep.

The kitchen's a mess from the cooking spree. I put the water on to boil for the grits and then wash all the bowls and utensils. I melt a dab of butter in Mama's iron skillet, beat five eggs, and cook them slowly to give them a smooth texture. Then I put two slices of bread into the toaster.

Mama walks into the kitchen, her head wrapped in a red paisley kerchief. When she sees I've cleaned up the mess and cooked breakfast, she grins.

"Morning, Mama. May I fix you a plate?"

"Yes, you may." She washes her hands and sits at the table.

I pour her a cup of coffee, plop some grits and eggs onto a pink willow plate. "Why aren't you eating?" she asks.

"My stomach's hurting a little bit."

"Sit down and eat a piece of toast," she says frowning. "You shouldn't drink coffee on an empty stomach."

The toast is burned so I scrape the brown off and slather butter on it. Then we bow our heads and Mama prays: *We take this food for the nourishment of our bodies that we may be better servants of Thine, oh Lord. Amen.*

She scoops a spoonful of eggs onto a piece of toast, adds a dollop of grits, folds it in half and takes a bite. I spread a dab of her homemade blackberry jam on the toast. It's tart, sweet, and purply tasting.

"Seems like you're turning into a songbird lately," she says.

"Songbird?" I say, surprised by that poetic word.

"I might be dumb, young lady, but I am not deaf—I hear you in your room singing songs I've never heard."

"You hear me sing?" I say a little embarrassed.

"Almost every night."

"I don't know diddly-squat about making music."

"Maybe music knows something about you," Mama says dreamily. She never talks mystical like that, but I remember that photo of her as a twelve-year old—standing in the middle of a dirt road. Head cocked. Dark hair, long and wavy. Eyes staring wistfully into the camera.

"Mama, when you were little, what did you want to be when you grew up?"

"Country western singer," she says, then giggles like a girl.

I envision my hymn-singing mama as a country music singer, and laughter spurts out my esophagus.

"What's so funny? I haven't always been your mama, you know."

"Anybody home?" Someone hollers from the living room.

Mama grins her guilty grin and hightails it out of the kitchen.

I gather my wits, walk to the living room, and peek around the doorframe. Holy Moly. BILLY RAY JENKINS is standing in his Navy whites on our front porch. Mama opens the door. He steps into the room. My lungs almost collapse.

"Billy Ray, good to see you. How about some breakfast?"

"Thanks, Mrs. Bridges, I already ate, but Mama said you might need a ride to the picnic. Can I load anything into my car?"

"There's a huge watermelon in the garden. You can put it in the cooler on the back porch."

He catches me as I peek around the corner, and I sashay into the room.

"Hey, Karlene." he says, blue topaz eyes glowing.

My eyes soak up the whole package of him. "Hey yourself."

"Mrs. Bridges, how about some ice to cool the melon?"

"Yes, that would be good."

He looks at me. "Want to ride with me?"

"Go ahead honey, I'll get the boys up," Mama says.

"Be ready in a minute." I rush into the bathroom and brush my teeth methodically, trying not to freak out that Billy Ray Jenkins is back in Red Clover. My face looks all smooshed from sleeping, so I splash it with cold water.

Billy Ray's eyes light up when I go outside.

"What you looking at me like that for?" I twirl around giving him a 360-degree view of myself in bare feet, raggedy cutoffs and Furman University T-shirt.

"You look adorable," he says, motioning me to go first.

We walk toward the sparkling white Pontiac Lemans.

Adorable? No one in this world thinks I'm adorable. He opens the passenger door, and I hop onto the seat. The inside smells brand spanking new. "Nice car."

"It's a rental, but it sure beats my rattletrap pickup."

We drive toward town. It's so hot, so perfect, sitting in this car with him, yet totally strange. At the intersection, Billy Ray stops and looks at me as if he has a thousand tricks up his sleeve. A horn blows behind us. He looks into the rear view mirror, turns around and waves at whoever the hell the honker is, then takes his own sweet time as he turns right onto Hwy. 200. That gospel group from California is singing "Oh Happy Day" as if Jesus himself had washed their sins away. I sit on my hands to keep from touching Billy Ray. His spicy spell makes me want to run my fingers across his broad shoulders in that crisp white sailor's shirt.

We pull into the Esso station that's deserted except for Gourd, the sweet hippie manager, who's sweeping the floor. Billy Ray walks toward the building, looking like a handsome young sailor, not like the boy who grew up in an ugly tan trailer a mile away from the world's largest cotton mill. Even with that crew cut, his looks kill me. Six feet tall. Olive skin. Straight, perfectly round white teeth. Juicy lips—soft as ripe plums. I close my eyes, tasting his lips. M*mmmm*.

"Hey, you," Billy Ray says, standing beside my door, smiling as if he had read my mind.

"Hey, yourself," I say, halfway embarrassed.

He hands me a small brown sack full of Atomic fireballs—my favorite nerve-soother. "How much ice you think your mama needs?"

"Two bags should be plenty."

"Promise me you won't go anywhere," he says, teasingly, and I promise. Then he walks over to Gourd at the ice machine and gets two bags and loads them into the trunk.

Now he's sliding into the front seat, and we meet each other in the middle. Our lips touch ever so gently, my heart thrumming like a golden harp. I nibble his top lip and then the bottom. Billy Ray moans and lets his head fall back, exposing his Adam's apple. Lightly, I stroke it with my index finger. He faces me, shivering with desire and we sit there staring at each other—I, the tempter and he, the temptee—our true selves leaking all over the place. Finally, I break the trance and scoot over to the door, hugging it dramatically. He grins like a toddler, his topaz eyes telling me so much more than words could ever say.

CHAPTER 16

If you don't eat it now

An hour later, I'm sitting in the back seat of the white Pontiac between the twins. Mama's sitting up front with Billy Ray. They're chatting like long lost friends. The windows are down and hot air gushes all around the car. I can't hear what they're saying. I feel like a dunce, sitting here—so close to Billy Ray—yet so far away. A sudden cramp almost takes my breath away. "Yikes," I say, without meaning to. He looks at me in the rearview mirror.

Mama turns around. "What's wrong?"

"My stomach hurts. "

"I'm going to quit buying coffee, young lady."

"Billy Ray, do you mind passing me those fireballs?"

He hands me the small paper bag—our fingers touch.

The twins hold out their hands. I plop a fireball into each one.

Billy Ray's old yellow pickup pulls up beside us, and his daddy honks the horn with a boozy grin on his face, then steps on the gas and hightails it on down the road. In the rearview mirror, Billy Ray's face has closed up on itself. I haven't seen Crawdad Jenkins since that camping trip a few years ago when he went on that owl-killing spree. Thank God Billy Ray took the shotgun away without getting his head blown off. Crawdad and Daddy used to be fishing buddies until Daddy got sober and quit hanging around with people who drank.

To get my mind off Billy Ray's troublesome daddy, I pick up my new *National Geographic* and flip to an article about koalas, kangaroos and wombats. Besides having built-in pockets, marsupials have other advantages over humans. The female's vagina is bifurcated, which means it's divided into two separate compartments in the uterus. Fortunately, the male's penis is bifurcated too. An image of a two-pronged penis flashes in my mind, which makes me realize Mother Nature is incorrigible as they come.

Red dust flies all around the Pontiac as Billy Ray turns onto the dirt road to High Mills Park. The High family built this forty-acre recreation park on the banks of the Catawba River so their employees could take their families for a day of old-fashioned fun. A paradise for lint-heads is what Daddy calls it. When the twins see the dumb little choo-choo train chugging along the riverside, they jump up and down on the seat acting like hiccupping frogs.

Mama gives them a double shot of the evil eye, and they settle down. I lean close to Mama, my pinkie finger barely touching Billy Ray's shoulder. "What time will Daddy get to the shindig?"

"Said he'd be able to get here by one o'clock."

"Why does he work so much overtime?" I say, prolonging the conversation—as my pinkie throbs with passion.

"Probably trying to make a good impression. And he's eager to make more money since Excelsior pays better than his old job."

At the picnic shelter, the twins and I unload the car. Billy Ray hauls the cooler over to the territory staked out by the men under three giant oaks—a place they can smoke and spit and arm wrestle in their undershirts without interference. The Al-Anon women swarm around the picnic shelter spreading the feast onto red-checkered plastic tablecloths. I spot my favorites: fried chicken, fresh corn, ham covered in brown sugared pineapples, tall fluffy golden biscuits, butter beans and fatback. My voluptuous Aunt Bette shoos her curmudgeon husband away from her famous chocolate silk pies.

Mama hands me a ten-dollar bill. "Honey, we won't be eating for a while. Would you and Billy Ray take the twins and let them ride the train?"

The twins skip along the wide gravel path, and Billy Ray and I saunter along behind them—our bodies close, but not touching. Gobs of people stream into the park. Families from Great Falls, Mill Ridge, and High Rock arrive with the same vengeance as the Red Cloverians. Some carry picnic baskets filled with home-cooked food. Others push hand-me-down strollers with fat sassy babies. Dozens of people wait in line at the concession stand to buy cotton candy, popcorn and corn-dogs. Two black boys in bright green uniforms sit on the concrete steps outside the Quonset hut that houses a two-lane bowling alley. One is sucking on a cherry snowball; the other's appears to be tutti-frutti. I wonder if they get bored to death picking up pins for white soda cracker bowlers.

The outdoor skating rink is draped in green canvas. It doesn't open until one o'clock. A vision of Billy Ray and me skating around the rink comes into my mind. I'm wearing a long white scarf around my neck and it's floating in the air. Billy Ray tries to grab it, but I skate faster, teasing him. But then an image of me and Spencer making out in the canoe flashes in my mind, disturbing my skating fantasy.

When we get to the miniature choo-choo train, Noah and Joshua both want to sit with Billy Ray, so he flips a coin. Joshua wins. Noah and I sit behind them. The train chugs through a forest of long-leafed pines around the perimeter of the park. I've ridden this silly train many times—I used to look forward to it, but today, my feelings feel sharp as razor blades slicing up the pale blue sky because I'm too far away to kiss Billy Ray's suntanned neck. This deep longing feeling reminds me of that crazy dream about a milky wave washing over Billy Ray.

When we get back to the picnic area, Daddy's cutting the watermelon. The twins run over and pull him down onto the lawn, like they're professional wrestlers. Daddy laughs so hard, he has tears in his eyes. Billy Ray shoos Noah and Josh away and pulls Daddy up by the hand.

"Long time, no see," Daddy gives Billy Ray a manly hug.

I put my hands on my hips. "It's about time you got here."

"Can't please that girl for nothing," Daddy says, rolling his eyes, then hands Billy Ray a slice of melon.

Billy Ray lifts the succulent red flesh to his lips and takes a bite. Juice slides down his chin, dribbling pink rose buds onto the white shirt of his Navy uniform. I dab at it with a napkin, feeling giddy at being so close to him.

Kelly's yellow taxi pulls up at the curb, and Billy Ray's mama climbs out the passenger side. Billy Ray runs over, opens the trunk, and helps Kelly and Teeny carry platters of food covered in aluminum foil to the shelter. As they walk past Uncle Floyd and Aunt Bette, my curmudgeon uncle whispers into my aunt's ear. Probably something disparaging about Teeny the Paleface hanging out with Kelly. People around here aren't used to seeing friendships between blacks and whites.

The only place I've ever seen blacks and whites acting like equals is at AA meetings. But Uncle Floyd doesn't believe in AA. Calls it a crock of shit—he's so dumb—he doesn't realize Aunt Bette's been going to Al-Anon meetings for the past year.

I walk over to Gloria Jean dressed in a lavender polka dot shift and tell her how pretty she looks. Wendell swaggers over and pats her belly. "Time to feed our boy."

"Hey buster, you might be having a girl."

"We will cross that bridge when we get to it." He wraps one arm around Gloria Jean, the other around me, and we walk to the shelter just as Mama's finishes up the blessing. "May this food help make us better servants of Thine, Oh lord."

I walk over to Aunt Bette.

"Why does Mama always say the blessing?"

"She's more sincere than the rest of us."

"Why is she like that?"

"One Sunday morning, the Holy Ghost flew into Lila, and that girl beamed as if a crown had been placed on her head. Most of us go right back to our sinful ways after we get saved. But your Mama's salvation stuck," she says, green eyes sparkling. "Now tell me about that boyfriend of yours. Looks like the Navy turned him into a full-fledged man."

"I don't believe in boyfriends, per se."

"Whatever you say, champ," she says, handing me a big fat piece of pie on a blue paper plate.

"I haven't eaten yet."

"If you don't eat it now—won't be no chocolate pie."

She's right. I sit down and eat the scrumptious pie, one tiny bite at a time. I spot Mama and Daddy sitting on a blanket in the shade under a large oak. They're facing each other, talking and laughing. Mama looks regal as Guinevere. Daddy jaunty as Sir Lancelot. Both ready to conquer the world. I sit there—my eyes feasting on them. And then, Billy Ray enters my field of vision—walking toward me—scrumptious lips glistening in the sunlight.

Please dear God—let this moment last and last and last and last . . .

CHAPTER 17

King of Siam

Billy Ray looks like Adonis on wheels as he skates backward around the rink. It's amazing how he manages to hold my hand, watch out for skaters, and dance rhythmically to Roberta Flack and Donny Hathaway crooning *where is the luv—where is the luv—where is the lu-uh-uv* as if it's eluding them at every twist and turn in their relationship. The lyrics are chock full of conflict, but the music sounds as if Roberta and Donny are cha-cha-cha-ing across the dance floor of a cruise ship sailing in the deepest, bluest waters.

But then Tony Orlando starts singing in that unnaturally happy voice of his to a girl named Candida whose bright eyes put every constellation in the galaxy to shame. Poor guy is a doofus. He even points out how ordinary he is—but promises Candida that their life will get sweeter the further they get from wherever the hell they are. WHEREVER the poor jerk is, he consulted a gypsy, who saw their future children romping in her crystal ball.

The song is lousy as hell, but the spectacular view of the tall handsome sailor skating with me puts me in a worshipping frame of mind. His woodsy scent floats into my nostrils and conjures up a vision of us wallowing around in a bed of pine straw, overlooking the

Catawba, all by ourselves, kissing, laughing, and doing whatever else strikes our fancy.

Later, at the amusement park, Billy Ray pinches off a bite of cotton candy. "Taste mine."

I open my lips, and he places the pink fluffy morsel in my mouth. We just stand there, staring into each other's eyes, but we get distracted by a ruckus going on out on the dock.

A man is up in Kelly's face, yakking away. I can't tell who it is.

Then he yells, "Goddamn NIGGER!"

Billy Ray sprints down the hill onto the dock, grabs the man's shoulder, and twirls him around. It's Crawdad, Billy Ray's daddy, his chest all puffed out. Damn it all to hell. Crawdad must have seen Teeny riding in Kelly's taxi, and he's riled up about it. I rush down the hill and stop at the riverbank.

"Well, looky here, if it ain't Preacher Boy," Crawdad says, slurring his words.

Billy Ray grabs his daddy's arm. "Let's go—I'll take you home."

"Who made you King of Siam?" he says, all high and mighty.

Billy Ray clenches his jaw. "I am your goddamned son."

"Whoopee-damn-do. Preacher Boy done learned how to cuss."

"Come on—you're too drunk to drive," Billy Ray says.

"Like hell I am." Crawdad takes a swing at him.

Billy Ray blocks the punch and twists his daddy's arm behind his back. Kelly steps in to help Billy Ray, but Crawdad breaks free and lunges at Kelly sending him backward off the dock. Crawdad splashes in right behind Kelly and flails around trying to punch him. Kelly quickly swims away and climbs the ladder back onto the dock. The water in the cove is deep. Crawdad splashes around trying to swim, but starts sputtering, and goes under.

Billy Ray just stands there as if his feet were nailed to the dock. His daddy surfaces, gasping and flailing around, totally panicked, and then sinks again. Billy Ray dives in, brings him to the surface, and struggles as he treads water and tries to carry all that dead weight. Kelly jumps in and helps get Crawdad onto the dock, where he flops around like a bloated carp, coughing and vomiting. Billy Ray climbs the ladder and stands on the dock, hunched over with fatigue as his Daddy pukes up the Catawba River.

Daddy comes up behind and places his hand on my shoulder. "I'm going to help Billy Ray. Maybe we can get Crawdad into detox. Can you help your mama gets things packed up and take her home?"

"Yes, sir." I walk up the hill, the sun shining in my eyes.

At the top, I turn around and look at the men congregated on the dock. Kelly's arm is wrapped around Billy Ray's shoulder, and he's whispering in his ear. Daddy sits beside his old friend, Crawdad, who is now propped against a post. And I realize there's only one thing going to cure that half-drowned man's thirst—and that's a monster-sized miracle.

CHAPTER 18

Boom shaka-laka-laka

Later that evening, Billy Ray shows up at our front door, wearing faded Levi's and a white dress shirt, his shirttail flapping. "Want to go to the river? I need to see water that's going somewhere."

I put my arm through his and we walk to the white Pontiac. He smiles halfheartedly as he opens the passenger door and then walks around and scoots into the driver's seat. We drive south toward the river. The sun is about five minutes from calling it quits—another hot summer day vanishing into another hot summer night. Billy Ray grips the steering wheel like the captain of a big sailing ship that's being tossed about by a strong wind.

"May I turn on the radio, *monsieur?*" I say to lighten the mood.

"Oui, *mademoiselle.*" He relaxes a little, leans back into his seat.

Boom shaka-laka-laka—boom shaka-laka-laka! The speaker blares. Sly and the Family Stone are singing their butts off. They're the jivingest American band ever from San Francisco—with a totally free attitude. *Boom shaka-laka-laka.* They want to take us higher and higher—urging us to own up to all our groovy sexual feelings instead of acting like we don't have any—which is exactly what I'm doing right now. Sitting on my hands to keep them off Billy Ray, who's probably too bewildered by his daddy's shenanigans this afternoon to even notice. I slide a little closer to him.

As we approach the Great Falls Bridge, the deep watery smell of the river fills the car. Billy Ray pulls onto the shoulder, stopping twenty feet from the bridge. He grabs my hand, pulls me across the seat and out his door. When we get to the bridge, he jumps onto the concrete ledge and pulls me up there with him. We stand and look out at the reservoir. "Do you think the Eye of God is looking down on us?" he says.

"Eye of God?" I ask, dumbfounded.

He stares out at the water as if he's in a trance. "A few years ago, we stood here, watching the sunset. You got all poetic, saying that God always knew our geographic location and liked seeing us standing on the bridge—being such good friends."

"I don't remember saying any such thing," I say, but my scalp tingles with the memory of standing on this bridge when Billy Ray put his arm around me for the first time. No telling what I said.

"Do you think God sees us standing here tonight?"

"I'd like to think so," I say.

Billy Ray grins. "Come on. Let's walk across."

"All the way?"

"You a fraidy cat?" he says.

"I'm right behind you." I push his shoulder gently and follow.

Heat lightning flashes in the distance, turning some clouds pink, others yellow. The whole night seems torn out of a science fiction book. We haven't even seen a car. I get this spooky feeling in the pit of my stomach that Billy Ray and I are the only people left on Earth, and as he walks along the ledge, I'm afraid he might fall off. So I look down at my bare feet—and scuffle along—my favorite refrain playing in my head: *Zealot for you baby, dreaming of your touch, trying to figure out why I love you so much.*

"Hey, you," Billy Ray says.

I lift my head and see we're halfway across the bridge.

"What you singing?"

"I'm not *singing*."

"You're humming and talking in between—sure sounds like a song to me."

"It's a little song I wrote a while back."

"What's it about?"

"You."

He grins. "Little old me?"

"Yes, little old you."

"Will you sing it for me?"

"On this ledge?" I say, my heart racing about singing for him.

"Let's sit down for a minute." He squats down and straddles the ledge. I straddle it too. There's two feet between us, so I scoot a few inches closer.

"It's sort of a talking song."

"Well, talk it to me then," he says.

I take a big gulp of thunderstormy air and sing *do-re-mi-fa-so-la-ti-do——do-re-mi-fa-so-la-ti-do* like an overzealous opera singer to help me relax. And then I sing it backward *do-ti-la-so-fa-mi-re*—holding the last *do* until I feel like I am swooning. Billy Ray plays along with my fake diva act—tries to keep his face serious, but he bursts out laughing. His manly laughter soars across the reservoir and echoes off the dam.

"You ready to hear the silly song or not?"

He nods. I open my mouth and chant

> *Zealot for you baby*
> *dreaming of your touch*
> *trying to figure out why I*
> *love you so much.*

> *When we first kissed*
> *I thought I would die—*
> *but I spread my wings*
> *and started to fly.*
>
> *You've owned my heart*
> *since the day we met*
> *I promise our love will*
> *never bring regret.*

I sing the chorus again, and a new verse comes to me straight from my solar plexus, so I sing:

> *Sitting on this bridge*
> *I'm afraid to look down,*
> *Our love's like that river*
> *I'm afraid we're going to drown.*

Billy Ray just sits there, shaking his head in wonderment. I can't believe I had the nerve to sing that corny love song. But I can't think of a better place to sing it than sitting here with him on the Great Falls Bridge—innocent as crickets—watching the moon rise above the muddiest river I've ever seen.

"Hey, Buster, let's go to Liberty Hill," I say, and he gets up and follows me to his car.

On the radio, John Fogarty's hot choppy voice wails about the bad moon rising—and rivers overflowing—and being prepared to die—which sounds preposterous to me, sitting in this brand new white Pontiac beside Billy Ray. No morbid songs tonight. I turn off the radio, enjoying the silence and the wind whipping through my hair.

The boat landing at Liberty Hill is deserted. Billy Ray backs the car up and stops a car length from the water's edge. He leaves the parking lights on and gets out. Before he has a chance to come around and open my door, I climb out and walk toward him. It's almost too dark to see each other. "You want to swim?" he asks.

"Sure."

He removes his shirt and pants, leaving on what looks like white briefs. "I'm going on in."

I strain my eyes to see his halfway naked body. Determined not to blow this opportunity, I take off my cutoff shorts and red sleeveless blouse, unsnap my bra, and step out of my panties, then wrap everything in the blouse. As I walk into the water, I wonder how much of me Billy Ray can see.

I call his name. Not a sound except the water licking its lips. My heart races as I listen to that voice in my head: *Don't be afraid of the dark—you sniveling little scaredy-cat*—but it's replaced by: *At what times I am afraid, I will trust in Thee*, the most useful Bible verse engraved in my hippocampus.

The water splashes like a giant catfish jumping—and there's a gasping sound. A few moments go by, and Billy Ray calls out, "Over here."

I swim over to where he's floating.

"Are you still scared of the dark?" he says.

"Guess you could say that." I lean back and float. My nipples feel like twinkling stars. The water coaxes me into being here right now—totally naked—floating beside a nearly naked boy. I wonder how our wet bodies would feel rubbing against each other. I want to tell him every cell in my body is tingling to make love, but I don't know what to do about these tingles, nor apparently do you, Billy Ray Jenkins. It's terrible, the way I've been raised—so damn *constrainedly*.

He swims over and whispers. "Are you okay?"

"I feel like a fire-breathing dragon."

"Cutest fire-breathing dragon I ever saw. Come on, let's go. Don't want your mama to call the Highway Patrol like she did last year."

"You go first."

"As you wish." He walks out of the river onto the bank.

I try to get a good look at his body, but I can barely see, so I trudge through the water and make my way to the white car, arms crossed, covering my breasts.

Billy Ray stands beside the car in his Levi's. His bare chest is so muscular—his torso long and slender. He reaches into the back seat, pulls a thin blanket from his duffel bag, and opens it wide. His strong arms wrap the scratchy fabric around me. My cheek rests against his muscular chest. My bare feet melt into the red clay. We stand together, swaying as if we're in a magnetic spiral being pulled toward the sky. He trembles as if he's about to have a seizure. *Boom shaka-laka. Boom shaka-laka-lak. Boom shaka-laka!* I'm afraid I'm going to make a fool of myself like I did that night on the beach right before he left for the Navy. "Billy Ray, I'm going to put my clothes on right this minute."

"Okay," he says, releasing me.

I hug the blanket and walk to the passenger side, breathing in and out, trying to un-blow my mind. I grab my clothes from the front seat and put them on slowly, letting the fire in my loins simmer down. Then I find Billy Ray sitting on the trunk of the car staring out at the water, his feet resting on the bumper. I hand him the blanket. "Let's rest awhile, look at the sky."

"You sure?"

"Mama was exhausted from the shindig. She's probably asleep."

He walks under a stand of loblolly pines, spreads the damp blanket onto a bed of pine straw, sits down, and pulls me down beside him. We lie beside each other, our bodies barely touch, giving my skin that electrified feeling. High up in the pines, a parliament of owls have gotten their feathers in a ruffle about something—hoo-hoo-hooting like there's no tomorrow. Billy Ray starts calling out the names of constellations, *Ursae Minoris, Ursae Majoris, Chamaleontis, Delphini, Orion, Leo, Scorpio, Centaurus,* and *Crux Australis,* which is Latin for Southern Cross. He keeps naming one after another, but I am distracted by how he smells—like cedar set on fire. He cuts his eyes toward me and says, "And I christen you as *Karlene Majoris,* the 89th and the brightest constellation in the whole Milky Way."

I give him a sideways smile, then look at the sky filled with billions of twinkling stars. I can't believe I'm lying beside this gorgeous boy—listening to the Catawba gnawing its red clay banks into mud.

Billy Ray sits up and looks at me. "I'll be going to California in five days, and it might be a year before I see you again. Let's go to the Blue Ridge Mountains. Hang out in Asheville. See the Biltmore Estate," he says, nearly out of breath with excitement.

"Are you out of your mind?" I say all serious.

He looks at me, bewildered. "Don't you want to go?"

"Of course I do—let's go tonight!"

He pulls me to him and looks into my eyes as his finger traces the outline of my upper lip, then the bottom. A shudder goes through both of us. He gives me a soulful kiss and I kiss him as if I haven't been kissed in a hundred years. I want to touch and be touched everywhere. I want to hear him say my name over and over. We begin to undress each other—and to touch and kiss each other gently—in every needful place. You're so beautiful, he says, his heart beating loudly against my chest. Over and over he says it, as if he means every syllable. After a while, I cup his hand around my *Gracious Alive,* showing him how to rub his palm against it ever so gently— which he does until the dark music behind my eyelids explodes into an infinite constellation of blazing white stars.

100

CHAPTER 19

Until you're gone

On the ride home, I sit real close to Billy Ray. He tries to apologize for getting so carried away. I tell him there's nothing to be sorry for, which is the truth. All we did was look deeply into each other's eyes, and caress, kiss and rub some of our favorite places. The rotten smell of Excelsior Paper mill zooms up my nose. "Ugh!"

"Smells like a billy goat's butt," Billy Ray says.

"Smells like a hundred rotten corpses with Clorox splashed on them," I say, determined to win the analogy game about the infamous aroma.

"One hundred rotten corpses? That is the *stinkingest* simile I have ever smelled."

I grin, impressed by his cleverness. I had almost forgotten the witty poetic part of his personality—but it's there. Lord is it ever there.

"Your daddy said he got a good job at Excelsior."

"One of his AA buddies got him hired, and he was thrilled to get out of the cotton mill—said there were too many triggers to remind him of his drinking days."

"Your daddy pulled some strings to get my old man into detox this evening—but he refused to go," Billy Ray says, grimacing. "I'd give anything if he could get sober."

My heart gets a cramp, but I don't say a word.

"That man's been worthless since the day he walked into Mama's life. Spent more time in jail than at home. She put up with his crap for years. It's a miracle she got the gumption to move out of that trailer. But Kelly renting her the efficiency above the taxi station is one of the best things ever happened to her."

"She's got it fixed up real pretty," I say, not wanting to mention the romance that appears to be developing between his mama and Kelly. I turn on the radio. Edwin Starr's singing: *War! Good God Ya'll—What is it good for*—which conjures up all those poor soldiers wading around in rice paddies, carrying guns, with love letters in their pockets.

"Too bad about Spencer getting drafted," Billy Rays says.

"It sure is," I say, discombobulated that he knows. "Did you see him?

"Dropped by on the way to your house tonight," he says, cutting his eyes at me. "Had to thank him for giving you those albums since you went all incommunicado."

"Oh, yeah, I forgot to thank you for *Tapestry*," I say, chagrined by my childish behavior. "Carole King amazes me."

"Karlene Bridges amazes me," he says sweetly, which makes me feel like a slippery fish released from a big rusty hook.

By the time we get home, it's almost midnight. I sit on the porch step beside Billy Ray, our bodies right up against each other. It's been a long time since we sat here with the porch light off and the moonlight giving just the right ambience. A musky aroma floats from his armpits into my nostrils, causing an outbreak of goose bumps. I wrap my hands around my elbows and hug myself. Billy Ray runs his fingers through his hair as if he's got a lot on his mind. I want to ask him what's wrong, but I just sit there absorbing the silence, satisfied to be breathing the same air after so much time apart.

"All I ever wanted in this world was to have a decent family," he says, sounding like a thirty-year old man. "I thought when I became an Eagle Scout, people would realize I was somebody worthwhile. Somebody to be respected. And when I joined the Navy, I thought my troubles would be over. Today, when my old man flailed around in the water, I hoped he would drown. I couldn't stand the thought of him messing up Mama's life or Kelly's."

"Is there anything we can do to help him?"

"Far as I can tell, there's nothing's going to help him except going back to his Maker," he says, a sad puppy dog look flittering across his face.

I lift his chin, make him look me in the eyes. "Forget about him. You're doing great in the Navy."

"Stay here—I'll be right back," he says.

I hate seeing him walk away from me, but I adore the way he moves through this world like a mysterious cowboy. He comes back with what appears to be an album wrapped in white paper. "Here's a good addition to your collection."

"Why, thank you, good kind sir."

He turns to me, cups my face with his strong hands. "I love the song you sang for me—and the way you sang it," he says.

A naked feeling overwhelms me. I lower my eyes.

His soft lips kiss my forehead. His hands release my face.

"See you tomorrow," he whispers and walks away.

I cannot bear to watch him leave, so I look down at my chubby toes digging in the red clay dust. He starts the engine and gravel crunches as he backs out of the driveway. I refuse to look up. I know I will see him tomorrow, and the day after that, and the day after that, and the day after that before he has to leave for California. But a surge of energy propels me off my butt. I grab my super-duper Coleman flashlight and run out into the street. He stops the car. I walk over to his window and lean inside. "Hey, Mister, we *are* going places, remember? Just like we always promised. No matter the obstacles."

A glimmer of the young Billy Ray shines from his eyes. "Yes—we—are—going places." He pronounces each word crisply. "You'll be the President, preventing ridiculous wars, and I'll be the Secretary of the Interior, saving forests and rivers. And tomorrow, we're going to take ourselves on a trip to the Blue Ridge Mountains for a couple of days."

"Or three or four," I say, standing beside the car door, my heart thrumming, feeling as close to Billy Ray as I do to myself. He kisses my lips so fervently—it gives me that gospel kind of feeling. I could stand here forever, being kissed by those heart-tenderizing lips of his. But I force myself to step away from the car.

"Go on now, skedaddle, I can't miss you until you're gone," I say all petulantly.

He smiles, gives me a crisp salute, and drives away.

I rush into the middle of the street, turn on the flashlight, and start making the biggest figure eight my arm can make. Over and over I use the light to make the sign for infinity. I hope he is watching me in his rearview mirror. I hope he is laughing his butt off. I keep making that crazy eight over and over. I don't think about how my arms ache. I think about that boy driving away from me. I wonder how, after all these years, he could still be such a terrific friend. I wonder how our bodies could rhyme so perfectly as they did tonight. For the life of me, I can't see any harm in it. When we're together—we add up to a big fat TOTAL.

CHAPTER 20

A parabolic painting

Mama's splashing around in the bathtub when I go inside, so I go to my room and unwrap the album Billy Ray gave me. It's *McCartney!* Paul's first album. I'm not surprised—Billy Ray loves Paul. The cover looks like a Japanese painting. A stark white table is placed vertically against a stark black background, and a handful of bright red cherries have been strewn across the tablecloth. And placed in the center of the table is a white porcelain bowl half-filled with scarlet juice. Several drops have spilled onto the white cloth.

It's like a parable—this painting. Makes me wonder who squeezed the juice out of the cherries—and how they squeezed it—and why Paul selected this particular painting. It looks like something Yoko Ono painted. I pull the album from the cover and a note falls into my lap. *Listen to Song 5, Side 2*, so I do as I'm told. Paul plays a dozen somber notes on the piano and sings *Baby I'm amazed*—which lets you know he's singing to Linda, the love of his life. He's amazed by how she loves him all the time, especially when he's in the middle of something he doesn't understand—probably his breakup with his Liverpool buddies.

But Paul sounds totally susceptible to love, which is how I've felt ever since Billy Ray walked into our living room this morning. Until he said the word adorable, I had *never* thought of myself that way. And the way he looks at me with those dazed topaz eyes wrecks me. It's like he's flipping through a Karlene and Billy Ray Catalog in his mind—remembering every moment we've spent together.

But Paul's heart-crucifying song is about to kill me, so I turn off the Zenith, grab the paper bag of Atomic fireballs Billy Ray gave me, and pop one into my mouth. Then to distract myself from thinking about our trip tomorrow, I pick up *Lady Chatterley's Lover* and start reading it all over again—this time I aim to find its redeeming qualities.

Mama knocks gently and opens the door, dressed in a white nightgown. "What's that you're reading?"

"An old English novel—nothing to get excited about," I say, carefully concealing the cover.

"You haven't read to me in a long time," she says, then sits on the bed. "Mind reading me the first paragraph or two?"

Holy Damn Moly. I can't remember how Old D. H. launched this confounded book. I cross my toes for luck and turn to the first page and read:

> *Ours is essentially a tragic age, so we refuse to take it tragically. The cataclysm has happened, we are among the ruins, we start to build up new little habitats, to have new little hopes. It is rather hard work: there is no smooth road into the future: but we go round, or scramble over the obstacles. We've got to live, no matter how many skies have fallen.*

"No matter how many skies have fallen," Mama says, her eyes glowing from a faraway place. "I really like the way that sounds."

I like the way it sounds too—but I am too stunned by D. H. Lawrence's near-perfect impersonation of Ralph Waldo Emerson to say a word.

"Is Billy Ray okay?" she says, her brow furrowed.

"Would you be okay if Crawdad Jenkins were your daddy?"

"That man needs our prayers," she says in her do-the-Christian-thing voice.

"That man is incorrigible."

She sighs deeply. "That man is lost."

"Good night, mama," I say dismissively.

She says goodnight and closes the door.

An image of Crawdad Jenkins' flailing around in the Catawba flashes in my mind—but I wipe that memory from the history of the world. I refuse to dwell on things I cannot change. I close my eyes and feel the velvety touch of Billy Ray's lips. I hear the awed sounds he makes as I touch him. The delicious smell of his skin zooms into my brain and blossoms into an outright epiphany: I am not some loosey-goosey, soft-in-the-head girl! I am an intelligent, hot-blooded American girl born with free will. And I've seen the truth in Billy Ray's eyes. That boy loves me to pieces. Either one of us could be zapped from this earth at any moment. To delay joy as well deserved as ours is highly unintelligent. Before that boy leaves, I will use every ounce of myself to love him.

I am only going to be Karlene Kaye Bridges ONCE.

He is only going to be Billy Ray ONCE.

Our time has come.

CHAPTER 21

The Wrong Pond

Billy Ray looked in the rearview mirror as he drove away from Karlene's. She stood in the middle of the street, making the infinity sign with her flashlight. He lifted his palm, sniffed for a scent of her, and shivered thinking about the sounds she'd made as his eager hand helped her climb some high mountain. He'd almost laughed, it made him so happy, but he knew where that would get him. Karlene hated being laughed at. It was the only time she ever acted insecure. He figured that's why she said crazy things sometimes—to keep people laughing about something beside herself. Tonight, though, she had been wide open and loved him as if she might never get the chance again.

Who knew what tomorrow would bring? For himself and Karlene? The next few days, he wanted to spend every moment with her. Tonight when she sang that song—about being a zealot for him—of all people on this earth—he felt a wave of hope about their relationship. Karlene was a zealot period—and had a bossy streak that was ten miles long. The first time he laid eyes on her, she'd been fishing at Sadie's Pond. A pipsqueak of a girl—a tomboy—like he'd never seen before. He walked up to her and introduced himself. Her fierce blue eyes looked him up and down, trying to decide whether she wanted to make his acquaintance. Then she proceeded to tell him that if he *intended* to catch any fish—he was at the *wrong* pond. The only thing in Sadie's Pond were turtles—lots of turtles.

He said he'd never heard tell of a pond being *wrong* before.

She laughed outright, then challenged him to a rock-skipping contest, and then skipped rocks across that pond like you wouldn't believe. They'd been friends ever since. Karlene loved being outdoors. Running. Hiking. Fishing. Playing basketball. Making go-carts. Climbing telephone poles. Her scars were interesting as a boy's. She loved words as if they had beating hearts. And she was curious about everything. He felt lucky to be one of the many things she was zealous about.

Earlier, when he saw Spencer's van in front of Flower Power Records, he went inside and found Spencer playing a new song about taking the high road. Billy Ray thought the song was worth recording and told him so. They sat around and talked—Spencer about getting drafted—Billy Ray about his life in the Navy. Then Spencer joked about how his old man had taken up housekeeping with Darla-What's-Her-Name. Billy Ray could tell Spencer was hurt, so he opened up and told him how his drunkass daddy almost drowned in the Catawba.

But when Billy Ray said Karlene's name, there was a flash of pain in Spencer's eyes. He could tell Spencer still loved Karlene—even more than before, but her feelings for Spencer were impossible to read. Loving the same girl as Spencer had almost warped his mind, but Billy Ray pressed on with the conversation, treating Spencer like a good friend because that's what he was. When he mentioned that he wanted to take Karlene on a trip to Asheville, Spencer recommended a hotel in Black Mountain that had red rocking chairs on the front porch that Karlene would love.

Being with Karlene today had made him feel terribly happy. The whole day seemed perfect—the food, the weather, the skating. The way she acted like they had never been apart. He felt as if he were floating above the scene, watching himself have the happiest day of his life. The way she put her arm through his and walked beside him so confidently gave him a spacious feeling in his heart, but an unsettled feeling in the pit of his stomach. He had three more years in the Navy—there was no way she could bottle up her passion while he was gone. And she shouldn't have to. Tonight, her song had astonished him. He couldn't wrap his mind around the fact that she wrote a love song for him and had the guts to sing it to him. Karlene had gotten bolder and braver. She was going places he could never even imagine.

Billy Ray looked out at the strange crossroads of Highway 200 and High Street. Everything shimmered with life. The bold steel steeple rising above Second Baptist. Dozens of shiny cars at the Jiffy Grill—filled with love-starved boys and girls—eating cheeseburgers and fried onion rings. Across the street at Red Clover Toyland—the giant toy soldier saluted everyone who passed. The soldier's uniform used to be royal blue and the plume on his helmet was deep purple—but the colors had faded to gray and pink.

Downtown, the only light shining was in his mama's apartment above Royal Taxi. He didn't know what would happen with his mama and Kelly—they were obviously in love. He suspected it before he left for the Navy, but today, his mama looked ten years younger. He did not blame her for loving Kelly. Kelly had been like an uncle and best friend to him. Billy Ray loved the crisp white shirts Kelly wore and the antique pocket watch he kept inside his black vest—a gift from Colonel High, whom Kelly chauffeured around for years. But no matter how well respected Kelly was, Red Clover was not ready for a love affair between a black man and his mama.

Then there was his daddy—showing his ass—calling Kelly a nigger, trying to fight him, and almost drowning. Crawdad Jenkins was still the town drunk. He'd been pickled so long—there wasn't a speck of light left in him. No one gave a damn about him. No one understood how insane he was. No one. And today, as Billy Ray watched his old man flail around in the river, he wished he would just go ahead and drown. Crawdad Jenkins was the reason Billy Ray joined the Navy. He wanted to get away from all the beating and harassing he and his mama had endured. But still, he ought to go by the trailer and check on the old man, who was probably unconscious by now.

When he reached Whispering Pines Trailer Park, Billy Ray turned onto the gravel road and drove slowly, veering around all the potholes. The place looked twice as desolate as when he had lived there. There were still six trailers, but half of them looked abandoned. At the end of the road, he pulled up in front of the small white trailer and parked behind the old yellow pickup he'd given his daddy before he left. He turned off the headlights and ignition, and sat in the rental car, looking at the place he'd lived in for six long years. A light flickered in the living room, probably from the television.

He stared at the trailer, feeling exhausted, as if he were at the end of a long, treacherous journey, but a happier memory swept him back to another Sunday night. It was freezing cold. He was sixteen, wearing a flimsy jacket, walking home on Highway 200 after one of his granddaddy's fiery sermons at Free Will Pentecostal. Karlene and her dad pulled to the side of the road in their old Plymouth station wagon. Mr. Bridges offered to take him home. Billy Ray said he didn't mind walking—that it was out of their way. But the way Mr. Bridges looked him in the eye and said, *Son, ain't nothing in this world out of my way* with such warmth—Billy Ray could not refuse. Karlene climbed into the back seat, and insisted Billy Ray sit up front. Then Mr. Bridges whipped into the Jiffy Grill and bought a sack of hamburgers for Billy Ray to take home. When Mr. Bridges pulled up in front of their godforsaken trailer, and his headlights shone on the duct-taped windows, Billy Ray was mortified by the tackiness. He thanked Mr. Bridges for the ride and got out of the car with the bag of burgers, glad to have them. Now, here he was again.

Sitting in the same driveway.

Staring at the same broken-down trailer.

Feeling appreciative of Mr. Bridges' kindness that night.

He got out of the car, climbed four cinder block steps, and knocked three times on the trailer door. Nothing. The door was unlocked so he walked inside. A horrible stench filled his nostrils and made him gag. It was not the usual cat piss, fried onions, whiskey, and dirty clothes odor. There was a deeper smell underneath the stench, as if the trailer itself had died. His daddy's half-blind Persian cat lay on top of the black and white console television in the living room that was broadcasting static at high volume. Billy Ray turned it off, remembering all those Sunday nights he spent watching *Bonanza*—pretending he was Adam Cartwright riding across the Ponderosa ranch—all one thousand acres of it—with his father and his brothers, Hoss and Little Joe. Real men living the good life, close to the land. But after Adam moved away to Australia—Billy Ray felt as if *he* had moved away to Australia—and couldn't watch the show anymore. Made him feel too homesick.

"Preacher Boy, what you doing here?" Crawdad said, leaning against the wall in the hallway, shotgun by his side. "You don't live here no more, remember?"

"Just wanted to see if you're okay. You almost drowned out there today."

"Ain't never almost drowned," he said, squinting his bloodshot eyes, as he lifted the gun and pointed it at Billy Ray.

"Where's your mama?"

"At home, asleep."

"Sleeping with that nigger boyfriend of hers. Hope they enjoying themselves. Ain't going to be no beds where they going." He cocked the gun. "I garant-damn-tee you, ain't no beds there."

Billy Ray took a step toward him. "Come on, Daddy, give me the gun."

"Your mama's a whore—ain't never been nothing but. And you—all dressed up today at the park in your little sailor uniform—mooning over that hippie girlfriend of yours. You barking up the wrong tree with that one. Nothing good ever going to come of it. I garant-damn-tee you. Nothing good—"

Billy Ray couldn't bear another word. He lunged for the shotgun, and as he wrapped his fingers around the cold steel barrel, a bolt of lightning flashed in his brain, and then thunder, thunder, all that thunder

CHAPTER 22

I'm a bluebird, yeah, yeah, yeah

I wake up grinding my teeth, trying to remember what I was dreaming, but the harder I try, the more the dream hides. Something about a hobo crossing a bridge. I look at the clock—it's six a.m. An odd thumping noise is coming from somewhere. *Peck-thump, peck-thump, peck-thump.* I look around the room trying to find what's making the sound and see nothing. *Peck-thump, peck-thump, peck-thump.* I look in the living room and discover the culprit. A bright blue, tawny-breasted bird is trying to fly through the small window at the top of the front door. I walk slowly and quietly into the room and stop about ten feet away.

I've seen all kinds of birds in my life: hummingbirds, seagulls, swans, robins, nuthatches, crows, cardinals, owls, hawks, sparrows, finches, woodpeckers, blue jays, and blue herons—but I have NEVER seen a real bluebird, its feathers azure as a blue flame. It's the most determined bird I've ever seen. Reminds me of that red-tailed hawk that flew into Mrs. Harrison's sliding glass door and almost knocked itself out. The bluebird *peck-thumps* once more and flies away. I walk into the backyard, wondering what the heck that bird wanted.

Mama's out in the garden in her nightgown—deadheading zinnias. Monday mornings, she's usually dressed for work by now. I walk over and touch her shoulder. She turns around and looks at me, her eyes, puffy.

"Mama, what's wrong?"

"Teeny called an hour ago. Billy Ray didn't make it home last night."

Seventy bells clang in my heart. "Why didn't you wake me?"

"Teeny said he could have gone to see old friends."

"He would have called her if he had," I say agitated.

"Your daddy and Kelly are out looking for him," she says, pinching off a withered red blossom.

"What about his daddy's trailer—did they go there?"

"I don't know."

"Well, I'm going there right now." I run toward the house.

Mama hollers for me to wait, but I take the porch steps two at a time, dash into my room, and change into my jeans and T-shirt. I grab the keys and head outside to the Plymouth. Mama's standing beside my car door, arms crossed.

"Mama, please step away from the car."

"Your daddy will be home soon," she says, her brown eyes begging me to stay.

I put a hand on each shoulder and push her sideways toward the front of the car. She resists with all her might, but I push harder. She stumbles, but manages to hang onto the fender.

"Mama, please get away from the car. I have to find Billy Ray."

She steps away, defeated. I race down our street, roll right through the intersection, and speed down Hwy 200 toward town. Everything's closed this early and not a car in sight. The Plymouth sputters down Main, and the light turns red at the High Street intersection. I stop the car. That old sing-along gospel song is playing on the radio—*Put your hand in the hand of the man who stills the water—Put your hand in the hand in the man who calms the sea*—but I don't feel like singing. A shiny black hearse glides through the intersection. Looks like Jamie Ledbetter at the wheel. *Dear God, please help me find Billy Ray.* The light turns green and I squall tires as I speed toward Whispering Pines Trailer Park.

As I turn on the dirt road, I realize I haven't been out this way in years. The Plymouth bounces through a dozen potholes as I drive past one abandoned trailer after another. But then, I see Kelly's taxi, Daddy's Fairlane, and the Sheriff's Chevy parked in front of Crawdad's dilapidated trailer. I slam on the brakes, adrenalin rushing through my bloodstream, and grip the steering wheel so tightly my knuckles feel like they're breaking through my skin. Then I see the white Pontiac!

I push down hard on the horn.

Billy Ray will hear the ooga-ooga sound and run outside because he knows it's me. He installed the horn when Daddy gave me the Plymouth. But it's Daddy who comes out of the trailer and walks toward me in slow motion. My soul feels paralyzed. He crouches beside my door. I stare ahead.

His hand reaches in, nudges my chin toward him.

"Baby, look at me."

I stare into his Jesus-on-the-cross-eyes.

"Baby, I'm sorry. Billy Ray's gone."

A little girl's voice whispers, "Where did he go, Daddy?"

"He's dead, baby."

"No!" I scream, vomit roiling inside of me.

Daddy helps me out of the car. I retch, but nothing comes out. I retch again and clear frothy liquid spews onto the ground. Daddy pulls a handkerchief from his pocket, wipes my lips, puts his arm around my shoulder and leads me away from the trailer—across the railroad tracks—into a meadow covered with blue, spiky wildflowers.

The meadow Billy Ray planted for his Eagle Scout project. I hear his voice whisper "Carolina larkspur," and then its botanical name, *"Delphinium carolinianum."*

I fall on my knees, my body wracked with sobs. Daddy sits beside me and lets me cry and cry and cry. After a while, my tears finally stop and I wipe my face with my t-shirt. "What happened Daddy?"

"We don't know for sure, baby—but looks like Billy Ray got shot taking the shotgun away from his daddy."

"His poor mama—does she know?"

"Kelly's going over there in a few minutes to tell her."

"What happened to Crawdad?"

"He's dead. Must have shot himself.

"Can I see Billy Ray?"

"No, baby. They just took him to the funeral home."

When I hear those two words, *funeral* and *home,* a tidal wave of sorrow swallows me because that wonderful boy had been searching for home his whole life. And then I realize it was *his body* in the hearse this morning—and it's probably laid out on a cold slab at the funeral home, being fussed over by Jamie Ledbetter's undertaker daddy.

I look up into the hazy gray sky.

My lungs heave out howl after howl after howl.

CHAPTER 23

Saw ye whom my soul loveth

O n Wednesday night around nine o'clock, I'm sitting at the kitchen table decorating the purple velvet armband I made yesterday. I couldn't bear the thought of wearing a plain black one like they wore in the olden days—so I found a scrap of purple velvet and adorned it with white lace. Now I'm sewing on little pearl buttons. One for each year of Billy Ray's life. Twenty in all. Mama's at Teeny's apartment, comforting her after the wake. Daddy sits across from me, flipping through the yellowed cellophane windows in his worn-out wallet. He looks up, eyes sad as an owl's. "You feeling better?"

"No, my stomach's still bothering me." I get up from the table, run to the bathroom, and have my fifth bout of puking for the day. As I wash my hands, the girl in the mirror stares at me, her bloodshot blue eyes asking: *Saw ye him whom my soul loveth?* I dry my hands with the fancy hand towel Mama put out for company, then wring it as tight as I can and fling it back on the rack all twisted up.

Daddy is still staring at the photos in his wallet, oblivious. The wind ruffles the red-checkered curtains, and I walk over and look into the back yard. It's pitch black except for the twins' flashlights beaming through the apex of the tent. Daddy helped them pitch the tent after Noah begged him to let them camp out tonight. Billy Ray was two thousand times nicer to them than I have ever been, and often took them camping

I turn and look over Daddy's shoulder as he gazes at my school photo from last year. My hair's flipped out nicely, and I'm wearing the same dynamite smile as my sixth grade picture. Next are Noah and Joshua's pictures, side by side. Every year their heads get a little bigger—Josh's dimple gets deeper—and Noah's grin a little more devilish. Gloria Jean's prom photo is next—she's dressed in that sapphire blue dress, her long, red, wavy hair flowing onto her white shoulders.

Then Daddy flips to the grainy black and white photograph of Mama cradling Gloria Jean in her arms with an emaciated cow in the background. Mama looks young and worried to death. It's when she and Daddy lived on John's Island near Charleston. I named this photograph *Via Dolorosa*—the Way of Sorrow. The last picture is a sepia photo of Daddy's mother and father on their wedding day. His mama's hair is pulled back into a bun, her face fierce and intelligent, her smile wistful as they come. His daddy's hair is parted in the middle. They appear to be young and rich and in love. Daddy just sits there rubbing his index finger across his parents' faces.

I sit down across from him.

"Know what my daddy used to say all the time?" he says, eyes blank.

I can tell he's in a trance—there's no need to answer.

He looks down and scrutinizes his parents' faces again. I drum my fingers on the green Formica table, feeling peeved by the pity party he seems to be conjuring up. How can he sit there, feeling sorry for himself when my heart has shattered into a thousand jagged pieces?

He lights a Camel and takes a puff. "My old man used the saying for everything. Bad crops. Bee stings. Impetigo outbreak. He used it when the blight killed all the chestnut trees. Hell, he even used it to explain Mama dying when I was a baby." He takes a drag of his cigarette and exhales a perfect ring of smoke, and then a smaller one that passes through the first.

"Are you going to tell me what it was he said or not?"

"Life is always right—son," he says, squinting as if he were looking all the way back to Georgia a long time ago. "Sometimes it just seems wrong."

I roll the words around on my tongue:

Life is always right—sometimes it just seems wrong.

"That's the most preposterous thing I've ever heard," I say.

He doesn't hear the anger in my voice—he's still entranced.

Finally he looks at me. "I thought my old man was a fool to say such a thing, and after he died, his words made even less sense. What could be *right* about him dropping dead while plowing the fields—when I just so happened to be AWOL from the Navy—drinking and raising hell." He jabs his stub into the ashtray, eyes glassy and wild.

"Where did you go?"

"I don't remember," he says, looking confused. "The point is that I wasn't where I was *supposed to be* when he died. And I didn't make it home until two weeks after the funeral. Since I didn't attend the funeral or see his dead body—I could not get it straight in my head he was gone. Every time I went home, I expected to see Daddy plowing behind Sparky, our old mule."

He takes another drag of his unfiltered Camel. "Not a day went by I didn't regret missing his funeral, and it wasn't until after I worked the twelve steps that I was able to forgive myself for not being at his funeral. I finally understood that life did not give a damn about my druthers. Life had to be accepted on its own terms."

"Accepting life's terms—is that another stupid AA slogan?"

He turns toward me, his blue eyes startled.

I walk up to him, my palm itching to slap something.

"Is that slogan supposed to help me accept the fact Billy Ray got shot in the head by his goddamned daddy in that godforsaken trailer? Accept they're going to bury him tomorrow under six feet of red clay in Memorial Park? Do you really believe I can accept any of this shit?"

Daddy stands there looking at me, eyes burning with hurt.

A car horn honks in the driveway.

"Halle-damn-lujah!" I grab my book-satchel.

"Honey, I didn't mean to upset you or—"

I stride out the screen door, the cicadas shrieking welcoming me to hell.

CHAPTER 24

If a kingdom be divided

I plop into Lucinda's Mustang, hugging my book satchel like a baby. "What you got in there?" she says in that lilting voice she's been using since the Earth stopped rotating on its axis a few days ago

"My Bible and a sick—call—crucifix kit," I say enunciating the tongue-twisting phrase. "Mama ordered it from the S & H Green Stamp Catalog last year and stashed it in the cedar chest. Looks like something a priest would carry around."

"Sick call crucifix kit? Mind if I see it?"

I open the blue velvet box, revealing a small wooden crucifix with a gold lacquered corpse of Christ and a tiny glass bottle.

"What's the bottle for?" she says, driving toward town.

"Holy water, I guess."

"My aunt uses the Bible like a Ouija Board—just opens it to a random verse, and lets the truth spurt out," Lucinda says. "Maybe it can give us some guidance about Billy Ray."

I pull out my raggedy white Bible with the finicky zipper, flip to a random page, and put my finger on Mark 3:23 which happens to be written in red. I read it out loud: *And he called them unto him and said unto them in parables, How can Satan cast out Satan?*

"What can that mean—Satan casting out Satan?" she says.

I shrug, then continue to read: *And if a kingdom be divided against itself, that kingdom cannot stand. And if a house be divided against itself, that house cannot stand. And if Satan rise up against himself, and be divided, he cannot stand, but hath an end.*

"What the heck is Jesus saying—that Billy Ray's family was divided against itself? That his daddy was Satan?" she says, even more confused.

"I don't know," I say, my soul aching for the truth. "Maybe Jesus is saying Satan cannot cast himself out of Hell—another force must be called upon. Probably that damn Holy Ghost." I read a few more verses to myself and stop at verse 29: *He that shall blaspheme against the Holy Ghost hath never forgiveness, but is in danger of eternal damnation.*

There it is written in red letters: eternal damnation!

Guess I am nothing but a big fat blasphemer because I believe Mother Mary is the Holy Ghost, the Holy Spirit, whatever the hell you want to call it. When I'm upset, it's her calming voice always telling me: *It's going to be okay Karlene.* But this time, I don't believe a word.

Lucinda pulls into the lot at Ledbetter's Funeral Home and parks beside Spencer's raggedy VW bus with a huge FOR SALE sign. He's sitting in the car waiting for us. I pull the cross from the blue velvet box and get out of the car.

Spencer escorts us into the vestibule where my friend Jamie waits, dressed in his mortician's outfit. He takes us into a dimly lit parlor. There's a dark wooden casket covered by a huge spray of red roses and it's surrounded by dozens of wreaths, mostly carnations and chrysanthemums. Their stinking smell makes me feel faint. I go over and sit on the burgundy sofa. Jamie sits beside me.

Lucinda and Spencer walk over and stand in front of the closed casket. She starts sobbing, but Spencer is quiet, his upper body twitching from trying to keep his feelings inside. I feel like a ghost, with no inside or outside. I clutch the gold-lacquered crucifix to my chest and pray for forgiveness for every selfish thing I have ever done regarding Billy Ray. Pray for his soul to have a safe passage to wherever nearly perfect souls go. Pray for his mama to bear her grief. Then I give the cross to Jamie and ask him to put it in Billy Ray's hands before they bury him.

My body feels huge as Alice's in Wonderland as I walk over to the guest book, and my hand looks miles away as I pick up the fancy gold pen and write *Karlene Kaye Bridges* as meticulously as it's ever been written.

CHAPTER 25

As above so below

In the parking lot, Spencer offers to take me home because Lucinda has a date with that new photographer boyfriend of hers, who inadvertently fell in love taking naked pictures of her. I tell Spencer home is the last place I want to go—I need to see water that's going somewhere. He steers the van down the long, curvy road toward Liberty Hill, headlights shining on black asphalt. The Weevils have travelled all over the southeast in this van—and it reeks of cigarettes, beer, and sweat, but smells better than those stinking carnations at the funeral home.

Spencer turns down the gravel road that takes us to Liberty Hill and parks near the boat landing. I take off Mama's red sandals and remove the little glass bottle from the crucifix kit. Spencer grabs a flashlight, and we make our way down the hill. A prickly sensation spreads from my feet to the crown of my head—as if my spirit were rising out of my body.

At the bottom of the hill, I walk over to a picnic table, step onto the bench, and then onto the table. Spencer sits on the bench. I look up at the twinkling stars, fling out my arms, and spin around and around trying to synchronize myself with the universe. After a few turns, I try to plant my feet, but teeter-totter for a few seconds before

I come to a full stop. As soon as my head quits spinning, I twirl in the other direction.

"Come on Karlene, get down—you're going to break something."

But I twirl and twirl and twirl as if I am a cyclone whooshing across the water—sucking up every ounce of the Catawba. Finally, I force myself to a stop. Then I sit down on the bench beside Spencer and look out at the channel Billy Ray and I swam in a few days ago, naked as babies.

"What was that all about?" he says.

"Just trying to get my bearings straight."

"Your bearings?"

"According to Billy Ray, that was my biggest problem."

"You and everybody else on Earth," he mumbles.

"We camped right over there a couple of years ago," I say, pointing to a thicket of pines. "Billy Ray's daddy got so drunk he ate flaming marshmallows right off the stick. Daddy and Billy Ray's mama got all liquored up and danced around the campfire until Daddy staggered into it—but Billy Ray helped get their drunkasses into the tents," I say, tears sliding down my face. "I should have kept him from going to his daddy's that night."

"Nothing you could do," Spencer says.

"His daddy was dangerous—and I knew it! He went on an owl-killing tirade a couple of years ago, and Billy Ray tried to wrestle the gun from him, but the gun went off and blasted a hole in the trailer."

Spencer takes my hand. "I need to get you home."

"I told you—home is the last place I want to go."

"Where *do* you want to go?" He squeezes my hand.

"The Harrisons, but I need to sit here a while by myself."

"I'll wait in the van." He hands me a flashlight and walks away.

Across the river at High Mills Park, the lights strung across the top of the skating rink look like a canopy of twinkling stars. An image of Billy Ray skating backward holding my hand flashes in my mind, and I still feel the jolt of energy that passed from his fingers into my sweaty palm. I look up into the black sky, studded with sparkling stars. Then I look out at the dark watery mirror of the Catawba, dimpled with the stars from above—as if it's reflecting every star back to heaven. A phrase comes to mind: *As above—so below.* I've always wondered what it means. As in heaven, so on Earth? I wonder where is Billy Ray right now—somewhere in between?

Something's moving over by the river's edge. I beam the flashlight. It's a turtle, carrying its green and yellow house. A river cooter. *Chrysemys concinna.* Awkward on land. Slow and easily confused. And I realize I'm just like that poor turtle. Trapped in my body. Trapped in my family. Trapped in Red Clover. And now, I'm caught in a trap of wanting Billy Ray. I bend down, scoop a few ounces of the Catawba into the holy water bottle and walk up the hill, wondering what in the name of God to anoint.

CHAPTER 26

Long Crazy River

On the drive back to town, the Fifth Dimension rhapsodize on the radio about how the Moon is in the Seventh House and Jupiter is perfectly aligned with Mars—and we're all going to have mystic crystal revelations—since we're now in the Age of Aquarius. Harmony and peace and love and understanding will reign on Earth. All we have to do is *let the sun shine, let the sun shine in, let the sun shine into our hearts, oh yeah*—which is absurd given the fact that Billy Ray Jenkins's head has been blown off.

When we get to the Harrisons', Spencer pulls into the circular driveway and stops in front of their house. I thank him for the ride and open my door.

"See you at the funeral tomorrow?" he says.

I shake my head, no-no-emphatically no, then get out and walk to the back porch. Mr. and Mrs. Harrison are sitting in wicker chairs, sipping red wine from crystal goblets. I open the screen door. "Mind if I crash here tonight?"

Mr. Harrison comes over with outstretched arms and hugs me, saying how sorry he is about Billy Ray. His kindness makes me wish I were his precious daughter—not the stubborn girl who skipped her best friend's wake, sneaked into the funeral parlor afterward like a coward, and cannot imagine herself at his funeral tomorrow.

Mrs. Harrison walks up to me and squeezes me against her huge bosom. "Hungry?"

"No thanks, I just need some sleep."

"Of course, honey. Clean sheets are on the bed."

I walk past the kitchen table, noticing the bruised magnolia blossom floating in a crystal bowl. Joni Mitchell sings on the stereo about how selfish she is and sad—and how she would like to skate away on a long crazy river. This whole day feels like a long crazy river I've been skating on for a thousand years.

I nuzzle between the lavender sheets, wondering how I could be so lucky to even meet the Harrisons. To be safe and sound in this lovely room in a beautiful house. And to have two very hardworking parents across town. Billy Ray never had *one* family devoted to him. No one ever gave him a special room in their house. No one ever called him *Jelly Bean, Sugar Muffin,* or *Chipmunk*—and now his body lies in stuffy coffin at the funeral home.

I close my eyes and imagine Billy Ray—*alive and well in California.* He's sitting in a classroom at the Nuclear Power School at Mare Island Naval Shipyard, listening to his instructor, but a silly grin spreads across his face, and he pulls out a sheet of paper and starts writing furiously—telling me every single thing on his mind—what the food is like—how it feels to be three thousand miles away—what the air smells like. He will enclose a photo of himself and his buddies and mail the letter tomorrow. In a few days, I'll find it in my mailbox. But then I think about his dead fingers wrapped around the crucifix, and a torrent of tears flows down my face.

CHAPTER 27

Catapulted into the kudzu forest

It's almost midnight. I stand in front of my dresser, gazing into the tortured eyes of a girl dressed in a black sleeveless dress. Shards of scripture lacerate her brain. *Ashes to ashes—dust to dust,* which makes absolutely no sense. And that ridiculous phrase, *certain hope of eternity*—any fool knows HOPE can never be CERTAIN. But it was the minister asking the Lord Jesus Christ to transform the *vile body* in the casket that makes her want to scream for a thousand years.

The poor girl picks up the scissors, takes a hank of her shoulder-length hair, and whacks off about eight inches. She grabs another hank of hair and takes another whack—and another and another until the floor is covered with strands of dark blonde hair. She stands there—hair sticking out like wheat straw. Not one strand longer than two inches. Her Frankenstein forehead, almost completely exposed. I have to get her out of this house before she stabs herself with those scissors.

Out on the street, the asphalt is warm under my feet. The lights are out in all the houses. People sleeping—pretending to sleep—or doing God knows what else in the privacy of their bedrooms. I've taken hundreds of these late night walks, mostly by myself, and dozens with Billy Ray, usually ending up at Bear Creek. As I walk down the slope at the end of our street, I remember how scared I used to get when the school bus careened down this hill. Afraid the brakes wouldn't work—and we'd be catapulted into the kudzu forest, and the vines would wrap around us, and we'd never be found. But now I turn and look up the hill, and see it isn't steep at all.

A light breeze ruffles the kudzu as I walk along the clay path to the creek. The musky smell of its purple flowers bombards my senses. People joke about kudzu, saying it will eventually eat the South, but the Chinese used it for centuries to cleanse the liver, treat hangovers, and curb people's cravings for alcohol. It's a shame that NASA engineers can build a multi-million-dollar lunar roving vehicle to drive around on the moon—but our doctors CANNOT find a way to cure people's cravings for alcohol before they go insane and blow someone's head off.

I stand on the bank of Bear Creek mesmerized by the moonlight shimmering on the slow moving water. The cicada's high pitched shrill puts me into a trance. I walk into the creek—my toes squishing in the red clay silt. I look up at the bright stars strewn across the black sky. Images of the funeral whirl in my head. Billy Ray's preacher-granddaddy choking up. Mama sitting on the church pew, one arm around Noah's shoulder, the other around Josh's—all three of them weeping their eyes out. The grim faces of the pallbearers, especially Daddy, Kelly, and Spencer's, as they carry Billy Ray's casket out of the church. Poor Teeny falling onto the ground sobbing at the gravesite.

And then last night's dream flashes in my mind. I'm high up in an ivory tower, looking out the window, as if I am Rapunzel. In the distance, a hobo walks away from me toward the setting sun, kicking up dust. He carries a bindle across his shoulder with a red bundle tied around the end. He walks across a high arching bridge and stops in the middle as he watches the fiery sun slip from the horizon. The hobo turns and gazes up at me in the tower. I can't see his face—he's wearing a hat. It's like he's waiting for me to go with him, or to wave goodbye—I can't tell which. It's the second time I've had this dream.

It has to be about Billy Ray—he loved hobos. Every night, he used to lie awake waiting for the L & N train to rumble down the tracks behind his trailer. He loved to hear it whistle its going-someplace-else song. Every time he heard it, he'd pretend he was a hobo who had just hopped on board. And he could fall asleep then—with his soul safe on the train. God knows where that boy's soul is now. But I know exactly where his body is. Buried under six-feet of red clay at Memorial Park. I tossed a handful of dirt onto his casket this afternoon and anointed it with the holy water I scooped up from the Catawba.

I cross the creek and walk through the parking lot of the Red Clover Motel—its old neon sign flashing *Red Clover Motel* one second and *Red Lover Motel* the next. Then I walk along Highway 200 towards town. The Jiffy Grill's closed, but the huge Schlitz sign burns bright as a beacon, which reminds me of Sunday night a few years ago. Daddy and I had just left church and saw Billy Ray walking home. Daddy offered him a ride, then pulled into the Jiffy, and said it wasn't a decent place for *a girl*. They went inside and sat at the counter, chitchatting as if they were father and son. I sat on the hood of the car, fuming. Later, when we dropped Billy Ray off with a sack of burgers at his trailer, Daddy seemed restless—as if a drunk were trying to crawl out of his skin. He'd been sober for months, but on the way home, he stopped by the bootlegger's house. Lately, Daddy has the same kind of restlessness. It's as if he blames himself for Billy Ray's death because he wasn't able to get Crawdad to go into detox that night.

I make my way downtown and climb the fire escape to the roof of the bakery. The fruity scent of purple petunias wafts up from the window boxes. Everything looks quaint as can be in Red Clover, but no matter how quaint it looks or how sweet it smells, this town feels like a crime scene. A bolt of lightning flashes beyond the water tower, accompanied by a fierce thundering boom. Rain would have been a blessing at the funeral today—the air, almost too heavy to breathe.

Billy Ray and I climbed up here every year to watch the Christmas parade. A couple of years ago, nickel-sized snowflakes began to float from the gray sky as Lucinda strutted up Main Street in her red-sequined costume. Billy Ray and I hollered at her, and she responded by tossing her baton real high into the air, blowing us a kiss, and catching the baton, then leading the marching band down the street. Overcome by the magnificence of that moment, I reached over and kissed Billy Ray passionately, as if I might never see him again. Eyes dancing, he asked what had gotten into me. I said I could not resist kissing him—with the snow being such an aphrodisiac and all. He laughed his butt off about that—the deep belly laugh of a grown man. I can still hear his amazing laugh.

Up the street, the venetian blinds are closed at Flower Power Records, but there's a golden glow coming from inside. Maybe Spencer's there. Another huge flash of lightning reminds me of that phrase Billy Ray taught me: *Lightning is always followed by thunder.* He said thunder was nothing but a shock wave caused by lightning, and it traveled at the speed of sound. Any time I saw lightning, I should start counting until I heard thunder, and for every five seconds counted, the storm would be one mile away.

Rain falls in heavy sheets a block north, and by the time I make it down the rickety fire escape, my dress is soaking wet. I race up the sidewalk to the record store, stand under the red awning, and stare at the green door covered with psychedelic flowers, happy faces, and peace signs. That old funky blues song drifts out into the street:

> *You better come on*
> *in my kitchen*
> *baby, it's goin' to be rainin' outdoors*

Robert Johnson sounds like he's been haunted by loneliness every second of his life. I rap on the door three times—my knuckles make a sound as fierce as a woodpecker's beak. Then I put my ear to the door. Robert pours out the truth with that slippery voice of his—that the girl with the crushed heart, standing at the door is lookin' for a good friend—*but none can be found.*

I raise my fist to knock again, but the door opens and Spencer's standing there in a white T-shirt and blue jeans. When he sees it's me, his eyebrows form little teepees. Maybe it's my scarecrow hair sticking out all over the place. Or the tears streaming down my cheeks. Or how that blues song mimics our situation. Him standing there—me standing here—storm coming. But then I see there's someone else in the store.

Maybe Spencer's raised eyebrows are not about *me* at all.

Maybe they're about Mrs. Crenshaw, the perky bank teller, dressed in the white shirt Spencer wore to the funeral today, her skinny legs tippy-toeing to the back of the store—her hand opening the door to Spencer's apartment and closing it behind her.

"Come on in." He reaches for my hand, but I yank it away and stand there looking into Spencer's apologetic eyes. I wonder how long those two have been having their late night rendezvous. Wonder what kind of bed Spencer has in his little apartment. Wonder if Mrs. Crenshaw bought her spiffy eyeglasses on account of Spencer. The bluesman keeps pleading:

> *You better come on*
> *in my kitchen*
> *baby, it's goin' to be rainin' outdoors*

Spencer leads me outside to the old church pew. We sit there barefooted. Spencer's feet are almost twice as long as mine and very slender. My feet are chubby and wide. Thunder rumbles in the distance while raindrops *plink, plink, plink* on the metal awning.

"Looks like we got ourselves a baby of a storm," he says.

"Definitely not the gully-washer we need," I reply, polite as a stranger.

"Mind telling me what happened to your hair?"

"Prefer not to talk about myself, if you don't mind."

"Ditto," he says.

Robert Johnson plinks and plunks on that guitar of his, singing about how his girlfriend is gone and won't be coming back, and I might as well come on into his kitchen before the downpour. It's like Robert Johnson's calling out from his grave. Telling me there ain't nothing I can do about anything. Nothing I can do about Billy Ray's freshly buried corpse. Nothing I can do about Spencer being drafted—or his affair with Mrs. Crenshaw.

I rise from the pew. "Better be getting home."

He gets up. "I'll drive you."

"No," I say firmly. "There's a lady waiting for you inside."

Spencer takes my hand, cradles it against his cheek, eyes sad as a hound's. Then he opens my palm and smothers it with kisses all the way to my fingertips, which makes my body shudder with sorrow—for Spencer—for myself—for Billy Ray—and for poor Mrs. Crenshaw, who's bound to miss Spencer's good loving when he leaves.

We say goodbye and I head home, a light drizzle falling on my shoulders. I think about how I've walked down Main Street thousands of times. Many times with Billy Ray, with one of us or both of us acting the fool. But tonight, I feel like a freak in a *Twilight Zone* episode, who just stumbled into a ghost town.

CHAPTER 28

Terrible Haircut Blues

The next morning, I wake up at ten o'clock—no one's at home, so I go to the kitchen and pour myself a cup of coffee. There's an envelope on the table with my name written in meticulous handwriting that looks familiar. I tear it open and read:

Dear Karlene,

Last night when you stood at the door, soaking wet with your terrible haircut, I felt so bad for you—and our situation. I wanted to comfort you about Billy Ray. And to spend time with you and tell you the next part, which you are going to hate me for. By the time you read this, I will be on a plane headed for Lackland Air Force Base in San Antonio. Everything got worked out a couple of days before Billy Ray died, but I didn't have the heart to bring it up because of his death. And last night with Mrs. Crenshaw being at the store, I didn't have the guts or the good sense to tell you goodbye.

I am sorry you are having to deal with losing Billy Ray and with the Harrisons leaving and Lucinda going off to college. And now, here I am, leaving too. Please forgive me. I would have stayed if I could. You are a strong person and a terrific songwriter. Please think of me fondly from time to time. I will certainly be thinking of you.

Your friend,
Spencer Jeffrey Randall

Damn it all to hell!

Another clever boy gone from my life.

Serves me right though—Spencer leaving like that.

Especially after how aloof I acted after we made out in the canoe at Sadie's Pond and when the phone rang off the hook the next day, I knew it was him, but I was too embarrassed to answer it. I treated Spencer badly, and I treated Billy Ray badly. Now they're both gone.

I must be the dumbest, cruelest girl on earth.

PART III

Crybaby Soup

Be not righteous over much;
neither make thyself over wise:
why shouldest thou destroy thyself?
Ecclesiastes 7:16

CHAPTER 29

Sayonara

A month later, on the Sunday after Halloween, I'm sitting on the Harrisons' kitchen counter in my raggedy bell-bottoms, one arm around Celia, an eight-year old version of Annie Oakley—the other arm around James, an eleven-year-old absent-minded professor. I can't believe how much they've grown. When I first babysat in eighth grade, they were little munchkins. Mrs. Harrison sashays into the kitchen. "Time to get your stuff in the car."

"NO-NO-NO!" they scream in unison, clinging to me.

She tries to pull them away from me, but they won't let go. She tickles James under his chin and Celia under her arm. They cackle like chickens and release me. She hands them sweaters and follows them out the door. My eyes wander around the kitchen. No copper pots hang above the range. No children's artwork displayed on the refrigerator. No more of Mrs. Harrison's homemade lasagna, or yeast rolls, or eggs Benedict, or Belgian waffles, or grilled pimento cheese sandwiches on her soft homemade bread. No more Beatles' music blaring during Friday night pizza feasts. Sitting in this bare kitchen makes me feel like a one-winged swallowtail.

"Hey, Champ," Mr. Harrison says, coming in from the den.

I can't bear the thought of my handsome pretend Daddy leaving so I look at the floor. He walks over, stands in front of me, and sighs.

I admire his shiny, caramel-colored loafers. He smells clean and woodsy as a brand new ship sailing out to sea. Images flash through my mind of the last few days we spent together in this house—packing up the last of their things, eating hamburgers and drinking milk shakes, listening to Marvin Gaye wondering what's going on in this crazy world, and singing *Never Can Say Goodbye* with little Michael Jackson and his brothers—even though that is what we were doing all weekend—saying goodbye without saying goodbye.

"Karlene?" he finally says.

I force myself to raise my head and look into his electric blue eyes. I try to be all stoical about the situation, but my lips begin to quiver. He holds out his hand, and I take it, lowering myself from the counter. He pulls me out the back door. My hand feels like a toddler's in his giant slab of a hand as we walk out in Mrs. Harrison's garden. The caladiums and marigolds Celia, James and I planted in the spring are brown weeds now. Mr. Harrison sits down on the concrete bench under the huge leafless oak. I sit beside him.

He lifts my chin and makes me look at him. Tells me how much they have enjoyed having me in their family the last few years, and how the children adore me, and how I am always welcome in their home, wherever that may be. If he can ever help me, or my family, I should call him at work. He asks if I understand. I say I do. He hands me a white business card engraved with the High Cotton Mills emblem—and his address and phone number in New York.

I pocket his card and thank him for the kindness he has shown my family and me. He tells me I am a champ inside and out—no matter what game I'm playing—or what the score is. He stands and tugs my hand until I'm standing beside him. Then he puts his arm around my shoulder as if he were my dad. We stroll to the front yard.

Celia and James are sitting in the back seat of his white Cadillac, singing she'll be coming around the mountain when she comes— toot-toot!

"Hey Jack, help me get this box in the trunk," Mrs. Harrison hollers, standing at the back of the blue Thunderbird.

Mr. Harrison jogs over, lifts the large box of books they selected for me from their library, and lowers it into the trunk. He gives her a quick kiss and looks at me standing on the sidewalk. My feet feel like they're stuck in concrete. He walks over, takes my right hand, and places the Mickey Mouse key ring in my palm.

"The agent said the house might take a while to sell, so if you need a place to get away, come stay here. Furniture's still in your room. Drum-set's in the basement. Bring 'em upstairs if you want. Bang the living shit out of them. Make yourself at home. I told the agent you might be spending some time here."

"Adios Amigo." I hear myself say chirpily.

He *adios amigos* me back, jogs to the car, and drives away. Celia and James look at me out the rear window, making that hello, good-bye wave of beauty queens in a parade like I taught them. I wave one hand. Whisk tears with the other.

"Hey, Ace, it's your turn to drive." Mrs. Harrison says.

"Mind if we stop by Memorial Park?"

"I'd love to," she says.

At the cemetery, I admire the perfectly formed pumpkin I took from Mama's garden last week. It looks lovely sitting by the white headstone—it's a small, bright orange one—so pretty and pristine. Kelly picked out the gravesite, here beside the weeping willows, twenty feet away from the duck pond, and paid for it. Members of the Upper Room AA Meeting raised money for the headstone. Mrs. Harrison and I stand there, her arm around my shoulder, admiring the white marble monument with praying hands chiseled above his name.

BILLY RAY JENKINS
Born April 4, 1951
Died August 15, 1971
Beloved Son
Friend
Pastor
Eagle Scout
Sailor

"Ye shall know them by their fruits." Matthew 7:16

Mama helped Teeny select the epigraph, and Billy Ray's preacher granddaddy suggested *Pastor*. I had almost forgotten how Billy Ray felt called to preach when he turned twelve, but later decided his life could speak for itself. I heard him preach on two occasions, both times about the Gospel of Matthew. I can't believe Billy Ray Jenkins is not on this earth. Makes me want to scream for a million years.

When we get to our house, the twins are playing basketball in the driveway so I park the Thunderbird on the street. Mrs. Harrison yells hello to Mama on the front porch, then grabs Noah and then Joshua and gives them noogies on their buzz cut heads. They acquiesce because they like her.

"Sit down a while, Mrs. Harrison," Mama says, fiddling with her French twist. "Karlene, honey, please get those fig preserves for Mrs. Harrison before I forget."

The kitchen linoleum shines like white quartz with flecks of jade. Mama must have been cleaning our little pigsty all weekend.

I appreciate her letting me spend most of my free time with the Harrisons. Guess she's trying to keep me from jumping off the Great Falls Bridge in despair about losing them. I pick up the quart jar of fig preserves with purple ribbon tied around the top and take it outside.

Mama sits beside Mrs. Harrison in the swing, telling her about this and that—and so forth and so on. I take the preserves and put them in the front seat of the Thunderbird, and then steal the basketball from Noah and make a perfect layup. The crowd in my head roars. I grab the rebound, dribble around the foul line, all cocky. Then I charge toward the net. Josh attacks from the right, Noah from the left, and we end up sprawled on the gravel with the ball nowhere in sight.

A whiff of body odor zooms up my nose. I sniff Noah's armpit—nothing. Then I sniff Joshua's, and it smells funky as a dead squirrel. Damn puberty fairy! I refuse to think about the horror of their adolescence, so I get up, brush off the dust, and wipe the pubescent smell from the history of the world.

"Lila, you are a rare bird." Mrs. Harrison rises from the swing.

"Takes one to know one," Mama says, standing beside her.

"Touché!" Mrs. Harrison says, then gives her a grizzly bear hug. Mama hollers for the twins, and they race into the house behind her. Mrs. Harrison walks toward me and my heart feels petrified, like the time I rode the Ferris wheel at Myrtle Beach by myself and it stopped at the top for what felt like hours.

Captain Mathilda puts her arm around me. "Let's get those books."

It takes both of us to haul the box to the living room. They've given me some of my favorite books from their library: *Tess of the d'Urbervilles, Madame Bovary, Anna Karenina, Walden, The Unquiet Grave, and A Room of One's Own.* Mrs. Harrison even gave me her favorite art book of Marc Chagall's paintings.

"Got something for you," Mrs. Harrison says, then reaches into the box, pulls out a white sweatshirt, and hands it to me. Emblazoned across the front in green letters is the Latin phrase: *Sapere Aude!*

I take the shirt, hold it to my chest, and suddenly I'm back in my eighth grade Latin class. Mrs. Harrison is writing SAPERE AUDE in giant letters across the board and then writes its translation: DARE TO BE WISE. She walks around in her spiffy red sandals, pontificating like Marcus Aurelius: *You are not a mushroom. You are a human being. A homo sapiens. You are a miracle. You are one of a kind. You are meant to be wise.* She stops at every desk and whispers something into each student's ear. When she gets to me, she leans in close and says, *You are an original, young lady.*

Now Mrs. Harrison is one of my dearest friends—and she's standing in our living room. I slip the sweatshirt over my head. It's soft and loose. Mama comes into the room waving a letter and hands it to me, grinning like a Cheshire cat. I rip open the envelope from Smith College and read the short letter signed by Dr. Oglethorpe herself in bold sweeping handwriting.

"Dr. Oglethorpe says I'm one of the top five students being considered for the Native Daughter scholarship. I need to submit an essay in late January, and I need to send an intellectual autobiography right away," I say, shaking my head. "I never thought I'd make the top five."

"Girl, just soak up the joy of it all," Mrs. Harrison says.

"She's right honey, you earned this," Mama says, and excuses herself.

Mrs. Harrison puts her arm around my shoulder, and we walk to the Thunderbird. She gets in, and I close the door. She wraps the royal blue scarf I gave her around her neck, and I stand there, memorizing the shape of her face, the arch of her brow, the curve of her smile. She turns her cheek, taps her finger in the hollow of her dimple like she does with Celia and James. I give her a little peck, as if she were my mom going to the grocery store—and would be back in a jiffy.

"Please think about coming to visit us in the spring," she says.

I give her a crisp salute, turn abruptly, and walk toward the house like a stiff-legged Frankenstein, determined not to look back, but after a few strides, my right hand lifts itself high into the air, and waves a backwards goodbye to the extraordinary Amanda Mathilda Harrison.

I trudge into the kitchen. The twins are at the table having a snack. Mama's stirring something at the stove that smells cinnamony. I reach for the giant Bayer bottle above the sink, shake out three aspirin, pour a glass of water, and swallow all three at once.

Someone tugs on my new *Sapere Aude* sweatshirt and I turn around. Joshua hands me his drawing of a sad-faced clown holding five purple balloons. And down at the bottom of the page in Noah's carefully constructed letters are the words: *We're going to miss Captain Mattillda too.* I am touched by the phonetic spelling of her name. When I look up and see the pained look on their faces, my voice box freezes. Mama sees my scrunched-up face, puts her arm around me, and leads me to my room.

"Get some rest, honey," she says and closes the door.

CHAPTER 30

Quirkiest of Keepsakes

L ate that night, I wake up forlorn and jittery. Everyone's asleep. The temptation to have a pity party is strong, but I need to stop thinking about the Harrisons leaving me behind. I need to focus on something positive like being a finalist for the Native Daughter scholarship. I need to write my intellectual biography for Dr. Oglethorpe, whatever the hell that is. First, I'll review my academic achievements. I walk to the living room, open the cedar chest, and pull out a threadbare red velvet hatbox.

I sit at the kitchen table and remove the lid. The box is crammed with Christmas cards, birthday cards, newspaper articles, church bulletins, birth certificates, report cards, and who knows what else. On top of the pile is the tattered White House Tour Guide Mama ordered after watching Mrs. Jacqueline Kennedy give the tour on television. Next is a front-page article from the Red Clover Chronicle heralding Billy Ray Jenkins, the youngest person in Red Clover to ever win an Eagle Scout award. He was sixteen then, his eyes wistful, standing there beside Teeny, with a million dollar smile on her face. There's also a photograph of Mama standing beside a huge zinnia blossom that won first place at the Shirley County Fair.

I pull out a manila folder with Washington, DC, 1969 scribbled across it in Mama's chicken-scratch handwriting. It's filled with newspaper articles. I pick up the *Washington* Post article where the handsome journalist asked me why spelling had been such a big factor in my life. Mama must have underlined my reply: *Spelling is about being precise, unlike almost everything else in the world.* There are quite a few congratulatory letters from dignitaries such as Governor McNair, Senator Strom Thurmond, Ruth and Billy Graham, and even Colonel Sanders. I put the folder aside.

Next is a photo of me looking like Little Orphan Annie with that frizzy permanent I got in fourth grade. Preacher Smoot stands beside me, grinning because I had raised one hundred and fifty dollars for the Lottie Moon Christmas Offering. No need to go through my report cards. Mostly A's and excellent conduct, except for eighth grade when I made a B in Algebra—and got a talks too freely comment from my Home-economics teacher.

The next keepsake—a postcard with a painting of the Ocean Forest Hotel—takes me back to the night Billy Ray and I walked on the beach after we danced our butts off at the Pavilion.

The hot salty breeze blows across our faces. Every song, every dance, every smile rushes through my bloodstream. Billy Ray leads me to a private cove, and we sit down and stare out at the cresting waves on the dark ocean. He starts talking in a gentle voice about how he doesn't really know what life's all about, but someone has opened up a door inside of him and filled it slap full of love. He says I am that someone—and I bring out the best in him. He's never felt so secure as he does with me. Only me. There's NOBODY else he wants. Every time he touches me, he feels—

I cannot bear another word. I put my finger on his lips, sh-sh-sh-shushing him. Then he gives me a long, tender, soulful kiss and I kiss him back, getting all worked up, but he pulls away from me. I can't believe this is happening. It's like I'm stranded in a No Sex for

Karlene horror movie. "Don't you want to make out?" I say my heart sopping with lust.

"Of course I do," his voice falters, "but we made a promise."

"Promise?" I say dumbfounded.

"We said when we got out of school, we would leave Red Clover and make something of ourselves."

"So, what does that have to do with our love life?"

"Nothing to do with our love life—just our sex life."

I just look at him.

"Having sex might mess up our friendship, or you could get pregnant. I will not be responsible for anything like that happening to you."

"I don't think it's that—I think it has something to do with your sweet sweet Lord," I say, mocking his favorite song.

"Every thing I do is between me and my maker."

"I appreciate that Billy Ray, I really do—but what you're *really* doing is spitting in God's eye."

"It's for your own good, please—"

"So you drove all the way from Red Clover to tell me what's good for me?"

"I drove here to tell you I joined the Navy and I'm leaving for Norfolk tomorrow. I am sorry it had to happen like this—so quickly. But I could not spend another day in Red Clover with my daddy carrying on like a jackass."

I felt like flinging myself into the Atlantic, but I stomped off down the beach. Billy Ray strode along beside me all the way up the beach, into the lobby, up the elevator, and to the door of the Harrisons' suite at the Ocean Forest Hotel, where I told him our so-called romance was over. He just shook his head and walked away.

The next day, he left for Norfolk. I flip the postcard over to a message written in my bold handwriting.

Dear Lila and Miller,

This hotel is fancy as can be and it's tucked away on thirteen acres of gardens and pools—a few miles north of Myrtle Beach. It has enormous oriental rugs, crystal chandeliers from Czechoslovakia, and a winding marble stairway. When it opened in 1930 it was one of the world's best hotels. The Harrisons say it looks a little shabby compared to when they spent their honeymoon here. I bet you would love this place, especially if someone else were paying the bill. Otherwise, it's way too expensive.

Your second-born,
Karlene

The weirdest postcard ever. You can tell something's afoot by the salutation. I wrote it when I got back to the hotel that night. The Harrisons were asleep in the adjoining room, so I paced back and forth, furious, repeating the serenity prayer, asking God to help me accept the fact that Billy Ray had joined the Navy, but serenity did not come. So I prayed for the courage to become my own person. To be more independent—especially from Billy Ray, the Sailor Man, and Mama and Daddy. That's when I wrote this postcard, addressing it to Lila and Miller Bridges—as if to obliterate their parental status. Funny they never mentioned the post card—and funny how it got tossed in this pile of keepsakes strewn across the kitchen table where I'm trying to conjure up an *intellectual* autobiography.

What the hell is an intellect anyway? I have been given some decent gifts, such as book-smartness, perseverance, and audacity— but all I can think about right now are my foibles. The temper tantrums, snide remarks, and selfish, immature things I have done.

CHAPTER 31

Psyche in pink sweater and braids

Wednesday afternoon, the day before Thanksgiving. I'm sitting in the cafeteria, choking down a cold baked potato, feeling entirely ungrateful. I couldn't muster up a smile for a thousand bucks. I'm working on the draft of an essay for advanced English—the one Ms. Flowers assigned two weeks ago. She calls it an exploratory paper. We were to make a list of three novels that stood out as especially compelling to us—and then reflect upon the protagonist's life in the context of our own life experience—and see how *we might have felt* under their circumstances. Maybe we would have an epiphany about ourselves or the characters or both. Ms. Flowers is really into epiphanies—not the religious holiday, Epiphany, but rather a profound and sudden realization about oneself or about life.

The bell rings. I gather my stuff, stroll into the classroom, and make my way to the first desk in the third row, joining the other advanced English students, who sit quietly—scrutinizing Ms. Zelda Flowers, in her pink cashmere sweater, short black skirt, and black flats, her long reddish-brown hair braided like an Indian's as she finishes writing today's quote on the board:

> *The purpose of power is to _____.*
> *Blaise Pascal*

Desi whispers in my ear, "She's wearing my favorite sweater."

Ms. Flowers turns around so fast, her braid whirls through the air. "Good morning, Mr. Sistare, so glad you like my sweater."

A few people giggle at Desi getting jacked.

"Mind reading today's quote for us?"

"The purpose of power is to blank," he says in his lawyerly voice.

"Blaise Pascal was a Frenchman, born in the 17th century. A scholar of the highest order. A Renaissance man. Mathematician. Physicist. Inventor. Writer. Christian philosopher. But please don't let Pascal's credentials inhibit your own bright minds," she says, wagging her finger. "Will someone please share what you think the purpose of power is?"

No one budges. It's so quiet, I can hear the big square clock ticking. I bite my tongue, determined not to be the first student to answer the question. Let some of the other bozos answer. The second hand twitches around the clock for ten very long seconds.

"Hmm—perhaps we need a little review. Will one of you cadavers come up here and write our Number One Principle on the board?"

Cadavers. Her sense of humor is punchy as Mrs. Harrison's.

Still, no one speaks or moves. It's like they're frozen.

I cannot bear it.

I stride to the board like she did on the first day of class and write: YOU CANNOT NOT PARTICIPATE.

"Hallelujah, Miss Bridges!" she says as I return to my desk.

"Now the rest of you, please take your pulse. Place the fingertips of your right hand on the inside of your left wrist," she says demonstrating.

Students press their fingers against their wrists, snickering.

"Now please raise your hand—if you lack a pulse."

No one raises a hand.

"Fabulous, now that you have confirmed you are alive—get out your notebook and write down Pascal's statement. Then reflect upon the word power. What comes to mind? Write down any comments that are stuck in your head. Any powerful quotes or speeches you've heard. Just write freely about anything that comes to mind. You have ten minutes."

Desi scribbles furiously across his notebook mumbling to himself. I open my purple notebook, write Pascal's statement, and my hand races across the page writing my favorite Latin phrase: *veni, vidi, vici,* and its translation: *I came, I saw, I conquered*—and then other random sentences as they ricochet in my head:

> *You could talk the stripes off a zebra.*
> *You ain't got a lick of common sense.*
> *Who do you think you are, young lady?*
> *You are adorable.*
> *You are an original.*

"Okay, everybody, time's up," Ms. Flowers says. "Take a few minutes. Look at what you've written. What kind of *power* do the statements have over you? How did the words make you feel when you heard them? How did they affect you—positively, negatively, whatever. Try to come up with three different verbs that fit into Pascal's statement regarding the purpose of power. Then come up and write them on the board."

A few minutes later, Alan the Beautiful writes *Control—Win—Govern,* which doesn't surprise me—he's captain of the tennis team, plus he's always been civic-minded. Next, Desi swaggers up, writes: *Control—Win—Succeed.* Jake, the Snake, our stellar halfback writes: *Clobber—Vanquish—Annihilate.* Deidre scribbles *Influence—Overcome—Rule.*

Next Patti McWhirter walks to the board with a sassy attitude and writes: *Control—Educate—Organize*. Patti used to be a wallflower, but somehow, she has transformed into a tall blooming cactus this year. And then it occurs to me Ms. Flowers is partly responsible for Patti's metamorphosis. Who else could motivate students to get off their butts on a rainy afternoon, the day before Thanksgiving, and scribble answers on the board in front of their classmates? No one, except Mrs. Purvis, our super cool psychology teacher.

I stride to the board and write my first word: *Conquer*, and then in honor of Ms. Flowers, I write *Motivate*. Another word tries to crack its way out of my skull as I remember the comments about how I could talk *stripes off a zebra*, but did not have a *lick of common sense*, and *who the heck did I think I was anyway?* And then the refreshingly sweet ones: *You are adorable and You are an original*.

The first three are putdowns.

The fourth an endearment from Billy Ray.

The last one a compliment from Mrs. Harrison.

But their *effect* is the same. They ENERGIZE my psyche.

So I write *Energize* on the board and return to my seat.

Ms. Flowers looks at the board. "What a fascinating list of verbs. Let's see if I can alphabetize them. Here goes: Annihilate—Clobber—Conquer—Control—Educate—Energize—Govern—Influence—Motivate—Organize—Overcome—Rule—Succeed—Vanquish."

"Way to go, Ms. Flowers!" Desi says like a cheerleader.

"But no one came up with this word," she says, writing PROTECT to complete the aphorism. Then she turns toward us. "Blaise Pascal said the purpose of power was to protect. Quite a few of you said the purpose of power was to CONTROL. Is PROTECT similar to CONTROL?"

Several people say no.

"How are they different?"

Patti raises her hand.

Ms. Flowers nods at her encouragingly.

"Control is when a person exerts some kind of force to get someone to act in a certain way. Protect is when a person tries to prevent someone else from being harmed."

"Excellent, Miss McWhirter. See how smart we are when everyone participates!" Ms. Flowers' grin reminds me of Mrs. Harrison. "Does anyone have any comments about the purpose of power?"

"Power is a major topic in the essay I've been writing," I hear myself say.

"Serendipity strikes again," she says, then sits down on the bright green stool in the corner. "Miss Bridges, will you please come up here and share your draft?"

"It's more of a rant because I got upset while writing it. It's only a couple of pages, and it's not polished at all."

"Sounds perfect. The point of a first draft is to get something down on paper, without thinking about the reader. Just write your heart out."

I walk to the front of the room and read my draft with all the gumption I can muster.

Reflecting on the Lives of Three Imaginary Women

As I looked back at novels I've read, I noticed there were an extraordinary number of tragic heroines, with Hester Prynne leading the pathetic pack. I am not using the word pathetic in a pejorative way—I'm using it in the strictest sense of the word. A pathetic person is one who is vulnerable—who arouses pity. But I decided not to focus on Hester Prynne and The Scarlet Letter written by Nathaniel Hawthorne. No doubt it's considered a great American novel, but it drives me up the wall with that morbid love triangle of Hester, her sneaky husband, and that adulterous preacher. Instead, I have chosen to focus on three 19th century books named after their so-called heroines: Madame Bovary, Anna Karenina, and Tess of the d'Urbervilles.

Madame Bovary was written by Gustav Flaubert, a Frenchman, in 1856. Anna Karenina was written by Leo Tolstoy, a Russian, in 1878. And Tess of the d'Urbervilles was written by Thomas Hardy, an Englishman in 1891, who gave it a ridiculous subtitle: A Pure Woman Faithfully Presented. But since all three books were written by men, I'm not sure any of them were up to the task of faithfully representing any woman, pure or otherwise.

These books are not for the faint of heart. Emma Bovary poisons herself with arsenic. Anna Karenina throws herself under a train. And don't even get me started on Tess. When Poor Tess was sixteen, she was raped by a rich boy, and as a result, had a baby she named Sorrow. But unlike Madame Bovary and Anna Karenina, Tess does not kill herself. She is executed for killing her rapist!

Emma, Anna, and Tess were born in different times. Birth control methods were lousy. The only real power women had was the power to ENTICE men. All three heroines were voluptuous, so men were eager to have sex with them. Except for their sexual attractiveness, all three suffered from a DRASTIC lack of POWER. They were pawns on the chessboard of their own lives. They had no political or legal power. They had little power to DECIDE anything about their lives.

They had been born into societies that valued only those women who conformed to the rules of male domination. When these women were confronted by someone they desired—or did not desire—like Tess with that creep who raped her, all three women were totally unprepared to take care of themselves sexually, emotionally, and physically. In 1971, things haven't changed that much regarding our education. No one teaches girls how powerful they are or how powerful their sexuality is. They don't teach boys about theirs either, as far as I can tell.

I stop there, my paper soggy with perspiration.

The room is quiet as a coffin.

Most of the students look startled. A few enthralled. Several look sheepish. Ms. Flowers sits on the stool, pensive as can be, but then she tosses her long auburn braid. "What an invigorating essay," she says and snaps her fingers. The whole class snaps theirs too, using our standard beatnik applause. And Desi chants *deep, deep, deep.* Others join in. My heart's aflutter.

"Thanks for sharing it with us," Ms. Flowers says.

"You're welcome," I say and walk to my desk.

"Okay dearies, for the rest of the semester, we will explore how power is manifested in the lives of fictional characters. And since you are the main character in your own life, you will explore how power is manifested in your own life."

"Ms. Flowers, what does manifest mean?" Jake asks.

"Great question, Mr. Schneider, your task is to look up *manifest* in the dictionary and tell the class what it means on Monday."

"Oh Ms. Flowers, that's an absolutely groovy idea."

A grin spreads across Ms. Zelda Flower's face, making her cheekbones even higher. The bell rings, but we all sit on the edge of our seats waiting to hear more about power.

"Go forth and have a groovy Thanksgiving!"

Replies of *You Too, Ms. Flowers* zing through the air. I'd love to talk to her about the Native Daughter Scholarship, but Desi, the Unsuitable Suitor has her occupied, so I head toward the door.

"Thanks for resuscitating the cadavers today," she calls out.

"Any time, Ms. Flowers, any time at all."

As I walk away, the stern faces of Sarah and Angelina Grimké come to mind, and I think maybe I could use the sisters as powerful examples of *real* women in contrast with Emma, Anna, and Tess, the imaginary "heroines" of Flaubert, Tolstoy, and Hardy.

CHAPTER 32

Her Pondering Heart

The fire roars in the Harrisons' stone fireplace as I sip Earl Grey tea, savoring its unique flavor. I'm glad this house hasn't sold. It's nice to get away from the hullabaloo at home. I can't believe Christmas is a week away. And I can't believe Preacher Smoot talked me into impersonating Mary for the Moriah Baptist Association's Nativity Festival. But I like sitting here by the fire, rubbing my fluffy fake belly, wondering how Mary must have felt when Gabriel showed up and announced that the Holy Ghost was going to impregnate her. Probably set her heart to pondering about the enormous responsibility of being the Incubator for the Light of the World.

I'd like to wear this pretend belly all the time—to keep me in the Holy Mother's frame of mind—but Mama's been scrutinizing me for abnormalities in my behavior, so I'm trying not get too carried away about this divine role I've been asked to play. Last week, I overheard Mama talking to Mrs. Harrison on the phone about my Mother Mary impersonation. Mrs. Harrison must have suggested I get professional help—because Mama said she didn't think I needed to see a psychologist. I don't think I need one either.

Over the years, I've grown accustomed to my bizarre ways.

I've also learned not to share my crazy dreams and mystical visions with most people. They don't understand what I'm talking about, and when I try to explain myself—it just blows their circuits.

Being a holy vessel agrees with me. I quit gnawing my fingernails. I feel relaxed and peaceful most of the time, as if the edges of my personality have been sanded away. Some days I still get the *purples*— those feelings that are ten times more intense than the everyday kind of blues.

But today has been a good day. I awoke early to put the finishing touches on two little baby quilts I made for the twins Gloria Jean is incubating. They're made from pretty scraps of cloth I stitched together with no rhyme or reason. Lots of purple because it's the luckiest color. I plan to sanctify both quilts by wrapping them around our little fake Baby Jesus on the last night of the festival.

Spencer's home from basic training—he called earlier. I told him about my Mother of God role, and he offered to bring his guitar and sing carols tonight. Preacher Smoot was thrilled, but the festival is canceled tonight because of the snow. I invited Spencer to come over after he has supper with his mama.

I waddle to the huge picture window, press my nose against the cold glass. My breath turns into a little puff of vapor. The oak trees look stark as fossils against the pale gray mist of dusk. Nickel-sized snowflakes continue to fall out of the silver sky. I wish Billy Ray were here to see our first snow and to see how hilarious I look as Pregnant Mary of the Pondering Heart. I'd hijack him and that white Pontiac, and we'd get the hell out of this little fake town of Bethlehem forever.

CHAPTER 33

Tonight in this cozy house

Spencer places a small cedar log into the fire, then sits on the Harrison's hearth, picks up his guitar, and starts tuning it. I don't know what makes him look so manly. Maybe it's the buzz-cut head, red flannel shirt, or his fierce eyes.

"Come on, Mother Mary, get out of that comfy chair, and sing your new song for me."

"It's too sad," I say, rubbing my fluffy belly. "Why don't you sing one for me?"

He holds his guitar high on his chest and looks out as if he's surveying a huge auditorium. "Good evening everybody, I'm Spencer Randall," he says in a deep voice as if he were Johnny Cash. "My first song is a cover by the American Breed. I need a drummer on this one and a back-up singer. How about you drummer girl, can you help me out?"

Spencer's a scoundrel. He knows Billy Ray and Mr. Harrison performed "Bend me, Shape Me, Anyway You Want Me" at my fourteenth birthday party, and that Mr. Harrison taught me how to play the drum part.

"Okay already, but I need a short warm-up." I say, then waddle over to Mr. Harrison's drum-set in the corner in my Mother Mary outfit, rotating my wrists and stretching my fingers. Then I pick up the drumsticks and do eight gentle strokes with my right hand—eight with my left, and then seven strokes with each hand—and so on—descending to one stroke. Then I repeat the process ascending back to eight strokes. "Okay maestro, ready when you are."

Spencer counts *One, two, three, four,* and I begin the song with that wild giddy-up beat. Then his guitar comes in and he sings in a rich raspy voice: *You are all the woman I need—and baby you know it.*

I echo: *Know it, know it, know it.*

You can make this beggar a king—a clown or a po-et.

I echo: *Po-et, poet, po-et.*

Spencer looks at me with those fierce eyes of his and sings about how I got him standing out in the cold and I ought to pay him some mind. Then he gets into the hard driving chorus telling me to bend him, shape him, any way I want him—then croons about how people say it's wrong for him to want *me* so badly.

I echo: *Badly, Badly, Badly.*

But he says he can't help it—he just wants *me* by his side—that I am the one who has the power to turn on the light. And as long as I love him, everything's going to be all right. He keeps begging me to bend him, shape him, any way I want him. And then, just like that, he ends the song abruptly just like American Breed on the record. My heart races with excitement, as if Spencer and I had done a real performance before a live audience.

"Come on people," he says, raising his hand to the imaginary audience. "Let's hear some applause for our deranged drummer."

I take a bow, then excuse myself and go to the bathroom where I unwind the duct tape from around my torso, releasing the fluffy pillows from my slender waist. It was ridiculous to wear this Mother

Mary costume, thinking it might protect me from my mushy feelings about Spencer.

I walk back into the den and plop into my comfy chair.

"Now, ladies and gentlemen, I have one more song to sing. It's written by Karlene Bridges, whose gig as the Mother of God had to be cancelled tonight. I'd like to dedicate her song to Billy Ray Jenkins, the man it was written for. Going to sing this a cappella." He puts down the guitar and sings in his laid-back, baritone voice:

> *Zealot for you baby*
> *dreaming of your touch*
> *trying to figure out why*
> *I love you so much.*

Then he sings about how I've owned his heart since the day we met, and he promises our love will never bring regret. I make him smile— I make him sweat—I make him feel unlike the rest. And when life gets tough, he thinks of me and his problems float away. Then he stops singing, cocks his head, and gazes at me as if I were the sun, the moon, and the stars.

"Only a moron would write such a swoony song," I say, feeling idiotic as the songwriter.

"Was it the song that made you swoon," he says, cocking his head. "Or the *way* I sang it?"

"I have no idea," I say, captivated by the intensity of his eyes.

He sits down on the hearth about three feet away. "Do you remember that snowy day a few years ago when you raced across my front yard in Converse basketball shoes and caught that touchdown pass I threw?"

"Yeah," I say, remembering how flirtatious Spencer had been that day and how I barely knew him.

"Do you remember how Billy Ray tackled you in the snow and you flipped yourself over and rubbed snow in his face? And then how both of you stared at each other forever?"

"Yeah," I say, wondering where he's going with this story.

"I remember it too. Stood there and watched the whole thing, like it was in slow motion. The two of you falling in love," he says, then shakes his head. "I wanted so much to be Billy Ray that day."

"You sure didn't act like it, scolding Billy Ray about not humping eighth-graders in your yard. You acted like a jackass."

"I *am* a jackass. Just like the night you showed up at the store after the funeral, soaking wet with your pitiful haircut. I felt terrible that Mrs. Crenshaw was there. I was so happy to see you and wanted to spend time with you. You didn't ask me a single question about her being there. We sat on the pew outside and watched the rain. And you just kept being my friend, which felt like a miracle."

"A miracle?" I say incredulous. "That's ridiculous."

"It's a miracle how we became friends in the first place. When Billy Ray left for the Navy, you and I had never really talked much, but you started dropping by the store chatting about whatever was on your mind. And you were always interested in what I had to say. You've been such a good friend to me the same way Billy Ray was. I've never met anyone like him—or *you*. You are wide open and hilarious. You make me want to tell all my secrets."

"No one tells *all* their secrets," I say, changing the direction of the conversation. "My song must have really choked you up."

"*You* choke me up," he says, eyes glistening, then turns quickly and grabs a poker and thrusts it into the fire.

That broad-shouldered, guitar-playing, flannel-shirted man standing in front of the stone fireplace makes me feel all swoony.

There isn't one particular thing he did to make me feel this way—it's more of a *total effect*. It's not every day a girl gets to hear an Air Force recruit belt out a full-court press of a song, asking her to bend him, shake him, and do whatever else she wants to do with him. And when he sang that zealot song I wrote for Billy Ray, it sounded true as if it had come straight from *his* heart. The last line of the song starts tickling in my throat just like the night it first came to me as Billy Ray and I walked on the ledge of the Great Falls Bridge.

Our love's like that river—I'm afraid we're going to drown.

Spencer leans over and places a log on top of the flickering embers. I am so glad he's here. Singing with him and joking around makes me feel perfectly like myself. He turns and looks at me with a halfway mischievous smile, and I realize Spencer and I are teetering on our own scary ledge.

But tonight, in this cozy house, we're safe and warm.

Ain't nobody going to drown.

CHAPTER 34

New Little Hopes

On New Year's evening, around nine o'clock, I open my eyes. The room's dark except for the small lamp on my dresser. Mama sits in the rocker beside my bed with her head bowed, running her fingers across the purple velvet armband I made after Billy Ray died—caressing the pearly white buttons I sewed down the middle.

I lie perfectly still, admiring the veins in her strong hands. She lifts her eyes, asks if I'm hungry. I tell her I am. Crybaby soup might hit the spot she says and goes to get some for me. I still feel feverish, but at least my tonsils don't feel big as golf balls like they did when I saw Doc Smith yesterday.

I sit up and reach for the December 31, 1971 issue of *LIFE Magazine* on my nightstand. It's the Year in Pictures Issue with the ugliest cover I've ever seen. The background is black—and it's crowded with dozens of big red words, such as: *Veterans. Drugs. Disney World. China. Dollar. Terrorism. Pakistan. Hot Pants. Jesus Christ Superstar. Demonstrators. Family. Gay Liberation. White House. Pollution. Jesus Freaks. Feminists. Unemployment. Nixon. Body Count.*

Too much drama for a girl with lousy tonsils, so I put *Life* aside.

Mama brings in a tray with a big blue bowl of oyster stew and a glass of ginger ale and puts it on my lap. The soup is covered with those cute little octagonal crackers. I spoon one into my mouth—it's nice and crunchy on top—the bottom soggy and buttery, just like I like it. I slurp a big spoonful of the milky stew. Perfect amount of salt, pepper, and butter. The savory flavor reminds me of something I've tasted before. Another sip of Mama's stew takes me back to that Ocean of Milk dream where I scoop up a handful of frothy water that tastes just like this oyster stew!

"Karlene, honey," Mama says, her voice bringing me back into the room. "I know this has been a hard year and I appreciate all the time you've spent with Teeny—buying groceries and taking her to Al-Anon meetings. I can't imagine how tough it's been losing Billy Ray and with the Harrisons moving and Lucinda going away to college, and now waiting to hear where Spencer's orders take him."

"We're all doing the best we can," I say. touched by her words.

We sit quietly, Mama rocking in her chair, and I think about the smoldering look in Spencer's eyes a few days ago at the Charlotte airport—how manly he smelled—and how delicately he kissed me with Lucinda standing right there beside us. I try not to think about him ringing in the New Year at Lackland Air Force Base in San Antonio with a squadron of buzz cut airmen waiting for their orders. I try not to think about how the peace talks broke down again in Paris last week and how the U. S. Air Force is bombing the hell out of North Vietnam right damn NOW. I pray Spencer will not end up as a crew member on one of those search and rescue helicopter teams he was talking about.

"Honey, would you mind read me the beginning of that novel you read me a while back? Something about the sky falling," Mama says in a young girl's voice.

"I don't know where it is, but I memorized the opening paragraph if you want to hear it."

She nods that she does.

I visualize the words on the page, and recite:

> *Ours is essentially a tragic age, so we refuse to take it tragically. The cataclysm has happened, we are among the ruins, we start to build up new little habitats, to have new little hopes. It is rather hard work: there is no smooth road into the future: but we go round, or scramble over the obstacles. We've got to live, no matter how many skies have fallen.*

"About a good a paragraph as there is," Mama says, dreamily.

"Must be good—I memorized it."

"Remember how I used to tease you about book reading being your religion?"

"Yes, it was right after I started reading all those books on astrology and the occult, and Zen Buddhism. They never mentioned the Lord—and you hated that," I say, lightheartedly.

Mama looks chagrined as if she'd stepped into a fresh pile of cow dung.

"You said I ought to get to the bottom of the religion I was born into instead of sticking my fingers into all the others like a Whitman Sampler. And that since I was born in South Carolina, God intended me to be a Christian. Otherwise, I would have been born in China or India or Africa," I say, squelching the urge to laugh.

"I apologize for being so backward."

"You don't need to apologize. It made sense and it was hilarious."

She scowls like child. "I was just being hateful."

I'm flabbergasted. Mama never talks about her shortcomings.

"I have always admired the way you dig into books—like treasure was buried inside every one of them. To tell you the truth, I have always been awed by how smart you are."

To think Mama has ever been in AWE of me is absurd.

"I failed first grade, you know, and was terrible at—"

"Lila Bridges, you are as smart as anyone I know," I say, determined to nip her slow-learner saga in the bud. "You are classy and practical as they come. You signed up for night school and you're going to graduate this year. You should be proud of yourself."

She rocks in the chair, her index finger tracing the U. H. R. carved on the armrest. Finally she looks up. "You know whose initials these are?"

"No ma'am."

"My daddy's, Uriah Heath Robertson. He made this rocker for my mother when she was pregnant with her second child, a baby boy named Heath."

"I didn't know you had a brother."

"He died the year before I was born, when he was two years old, but I didn't find out about him until after Mama died—and that's when I realized I had been living in his tiny shadow my whole life. Mama tried to kill her sorrow by cooking, cleaning, canning vegetables, sewing clothes, butchering hogs, wringing chicken's necks, and plowing the fields. And I was the one who ran around trying to cheer her up, even after I got married," Mama says, her eyes wistful. "Until we had that big falling out."

"What happened?"

"The day I found out I was pregnant with Gloria Jean I could not wait to tell Mama. We lived about a mile away in Aunt Sadie's cottage. Your daddy was at work, so early that evening I walked over to Mama's house to tell her about the baby. It had just started to snow. I was so excited, but when I opened the back door—I could tell Mama was in one of those dark moods—wearing that mad-at-the-world frown of hers. She asked me what in the world had brought Miss Scaredy Cat out after dark. I looked into her pale gray eyes and told her I was three months pregnant. She stared at my belly in disgust, then scolded me about how I should have gotten a job, saved some money and bought a house in town—and that if I had a lick of sense, I would never have married Miller Bridges," she says, with a faraway look in her eyes.

I look at the woman rocking in the chair beside me. A woman who is both here and not here—tangled in the past as she is. I conjure her up as a nineteen-year old woman with curves in all the right places and a curious smile whose heart got stolen by a good-looking, sweet-talking, thirsty sailor from Georgia.

Mama comes over, sits on the edge of my bed, and looks at me with those deep-set hazel eyes of hers. "Honey, we've never talked about sex or making love. I didn't know what to say. You're so smart, I figured you knew everything you needed to know. And that you and Mrs. Harrison had discussed it, as close as you are. Is there anything you'd like to discuss?"

A part of me wants to discuss *everything* with Mama, but another part of me feels it's a private matter. "No ma'am, Mrs. Harrison coached me on the ins and outs, and I had a gynecological exam with Doc Smith last month and got on the pill," I say feeling surprisingly relaxed, but then think I shouldn't let her off the hook so easily. "Unless there's something you'd like to say about your experience making love."

A halfway devilish look comes into her eyes. "Well, honey, I never had but one lover and that's your daddy—and I'm happy to say that since he got sober, making love is a whole lot more fun."

"Fun?" I say, charmed to the gills.

"Yes, fun. Anything else you'd like to know?"

"What did you say to your mama after she insulted you about marrying Daddy?"

"I told her to mind her own business. She was not in charge of me and Miller, or my baby—or anything else in my life. That's when she shook her long skinny finger and said: 'Lila Mae Robertson—you don't have enough sense to raise a baby." Mama pauses. My grandma's words punch me in the gut.

"What did you do then?"

"I ran out the back door into the freezing cold, looked up into the night sky, and calmed myself down by letting snowflakes fall on my face. Then I got down on my knees in the snow and begged God to give me enough sense to raise my baby. When I stood up, she was looking at me from the kitchen window. Then Daddy came outside—he'd heard us arguing. He cranked up his old Ford and took me home. I invited him to come inside, but he said he needed to get back home. I walked into Aunt Sadie's little house, proud as a peacock and threw another log into the cook stove. Then I baked a pone of cornbread, slathered it with butter and honey—ate one piece for myself—and one for my baby," she says, her face aglow with triumph. "It was scrumptious. I am telling you. Scrumptious."

"What about Gloria Jean? Didn't your mama love her to pieces?"

"Of course. Mama was crazy about babies and puppy dogs."

"Please tell me more about—"

"Shush," she says, pressing her finger against my lip. "You're sick honey, get some rest. Tomorrow, we'll have ourselves a brand new year."

Mama has never touched my lips.

Or shushed me like a child.

It feels marvelous.

CHAPTER 35

That day at the fountain

February 3, 1972

Dear Captain Mathilda,

Your erudite admirer turned eighteen yesterday—that's 6575 days of being a homo sapiens. It was dreary outside, and I did not want to wake up, but Daddy rousted me out of bed and took me outside to see the 1968 zenith blue Volkswagen Beetle he bought in Darlington at the car auction. I tried to pay for half of it, out of my get-out-of-Red-Clover-fund, but he and Mama wouldn't hear of it. I named the car Samantha.

Last night, Gloria Jean and Wendell had a birthday supper for me at their new split-level house that Wendell's construction company built. Lucinda drove up from Clemson. Teeny and Kelly came too. Everybody brought food. We had fried chicken, creamed corn, macaroni and cheese, turnip greens and cornbread. Gloria Jean baked a pound cake with caramel icing, which was scrumptious. Gloria Jean and Wendell gave me a portable black and white television for my room so I could watch Johnny Carson make light of this world. Kelly gave me a book, Trumpet of Conscience, written by Reverend King. Spencer sent me a tambourine, which he says is the most underestimated instrument. But the biggest surprise was from Teeny. She gave me a photo of Billy Ray and me playing in the fountain at High Mills Park. I had never seen it. When I opened the box and saw it there in a silver frame, alligator tears gushed from my eyes. Teeny almost hugged the life out of me as if she were hugging Billy Ray and me.

Doc Smith delivered sad news to Gloria Jean—she is NOT going to have twins. He called it the vanishing twin syndrome. Said it happens a lot! Gloria Jean is torn up about it. Wendell is acting stoical about the situation. But Gloria Jean still looks like she's carrying a baby hippopotamus inside her. I've been researching the birth weight of humans. The largest, a boy, weighed 26 pounds. The mother was a giantess from Nova Scotia, who weighed 509 pounds and stood 7 feet, 9 inches tall. The father, a Confederate captain from Kentucky, was the same height as the mother, but he weighed 30 pounds less than she did. How those two giants found each other is a mystery. It's a long way from Kentucky to Nova Scotia.

But since Gloria Jean is 5 feet, 4 inches tall and weighed 105 pounds before she got knocked up, and Wendell is 5 feet, 10 inches tall and weighs 155 pounds, I pray for a normal baby, a healthy happy girl, weighing six pounds or thereabouts. The expected date of my niece is March 28. Wendell gets mad at me for calling the baby my niece. I get mad at him for calling the baby his son. Our aggravation is 100% mutual. Please keep your fingers and toes crossed for a healthy girl!

Longingly yours,
Karlene

P.S. Thank you for the suede jacket you sent for my birthday. I love the long fringes and that golden tan color. Wearing it makes me feel spunky as Annie Oakley.

I stuff the letter into an envelope, then pick up the silver framed photograph Teeny gave me, and stretch out onto the white chenille bedspread, holding the photo close to my heart. I've memorized every detail of this photo. Billy Ray is fourteen or fifteen—I must be eleven or twelve. You can only see our backs and a glimpse of our profiles. Smack dab in the middle of the photo is that glorious fountain at High Mills Park—spewing like a geyser. Billy Ray and I sit on opposite sides of the oval-shaped fountain in our swimsuits. He sits way over on the right side—I'm way over on the left. We're as far apart as we can be, our feet dangling in the water. My body is turned toward the fountain, my hand reaching out to feel the spray. Billy Ray is turned in my direction, and he's looking directly at me—not the fountain.

I'm swept back to that day. I can feel the sun burning my back, cool water sprinkling my arms, and my puffy breasts swelling out of my swimsuit like muffins. I glance sideways and catch Billy Ray staring at me. Our eyes capture each other's—and there's this lightning bolt connection between us. Then someone hollers out Billy Ray's name. He doesn't blink an eye, just keeps gazing at me. Whoever hollered, hollers again, louder. Billy Ray grimaces and keeps eye contact, but the person hollers again, and Billy ray turns to see who's calling him. The lightning bolt connection vanishes, and I feel like a scorched lovesick girl.

I don't know who called out to Billy Ray that day. I don't know who snapped this photograph. It's as if the Eye of God captured the moment of an innocent girl flirting with a wonderful boy for the first time. A boy who's been dead going on seven months now. And now, the girl is totally and irrevocably grown-up. She's a young woman with carnal knowledge of the sweetest variety, who woke up this morning and felt sorry for herself because she could not see the man who thrills her to the bone with his good loving.

I grab the new Hohner Super Chromonica Mama gave me for Christmas—the one I circled in the *S & H Green Stamps Idea Book of Distinguished Merchandise* that costs four books of stamps. I suck on it, making a sharp sound. Then I blow into it softly, making a tender sound. I continue to suck and blow as if it were the bellows of Life itself.

After a while, I settle down and start playing "Requiem," a song that popped into my head a few weeks before Christmas when I thought about that terrible, awful, no-good Christmas when Daddy passed out in the living room and Billy Ray came over and baked sugar cookies with me. It's the song I avoided singing to Spencer at the Harrisons' that night, but I sang it to him the night before he left.

As I play the tune, a choir sings the lyrics in my head:

> *To whom does it belong—this sorrow*
> *this undreamable dream*
> *this ghastly wound?*
>
> *To whom does it belong—this sorrow*
> *Is it yours*
> *Is it mine*
> *Is it theirs*
> *Is it ours?*

I play it again and when it gets to the second verse, another choir kicks in and sings the first verse—asking to whom the sorrow belongs, turning the song into a *bona fide* round. The timing of both choirs is impeccable—and with all those hard questions being asked by different voices at different times—the song *doesn't* sound like a sad lonely blackbird singing in the dead of night. It's like the song itself is telling me it *needs* to be sung over and over in a round—because sorrow is not singular and needs to be shared.

But the other verses I wrote don't seem to belong in this particular song. They're way too flowery. But I love the personification in them, especially when the sky refuses to claim the sorrow, but offers up her blue space for red kites to dance in—and when the earth says she can't bear the weight of all that sorrow and begs the wind to scatter it across the weeping planet. But the best verse is when the ocean steps up and saves the day, promising to swallow the rest of the sorrow in tiny tiny gulps, so that the sun will quit fretting, and remember why it's shining in the first place.

CHAPTER 36

Bellyaching at the Bakery

There's something about this sugary smelling bakery that tears me up lately. I don't know why. I've collected some of my happiest memories here. Waiting for Daddy to get out of AA meetings, playing checkers with Billy Ray, and drinking coffee with Spencer. Kelly walks in and pulls up a chair. "What's gnawing at you, Miss K?"

"I've been in a twitchy mood ever since Teeny asked me to speak on Youth Sunday to celebrate Billy Ray's birthday."

"Why not talk about what made Billy Ray Billy Ray? Let people know what he was really like. What made his heart sing? Tell them about the summer he carried that red leather Bible around everywhere he went."

"Yeah—he sure was hung up on the Book of Matthew."

"Well there you have it, talk about that!"

Daddy strolls in, pours himself a cup of coffee, "Talk about what?"

"I don't believe that's any of your business," I say flippantly.

"You still bellyaching about giving that speech at Free Will?"

"Speaking of speakers," Kelly says, winking. "We need one."

"What about Roy?" Daddy says, eyes wild with fear.

"Said he had the laryngitis."

"No way, I am not prepared!"

"Just stand up there and tell your story," Kelly says.

Daddy scowls at his devious sponsor, then turns to me.

"If you want to see your daddy make a fool of himself, come upstairs in fifteen minutes."

By the time I slip into the back row, about twenty-five people have gathered in the Upper Room. Most are regulars, who work at the cotton mill, foundry, or paper mill. There's also an old farmer, a butcher from Winn-Dixie, and that gregarious woman who works with Gloria Jean at Catawba Insurance. The preliminary part of the meeting is over. Kelly stands at the lectern. "Please welcome our speaker, my friend Miller."

Daddy walks to the front and everyone calls out *Welcome, Miller.* He stands at the lectern—a tall, clean-shaven man—his reddish-brown hair slicked back like a movie star's. "I'd like to congratulate my friend Kelly for finally backing me into a corner and making me get up here," he says and takes a sip of water.

"Glad you're here," members call out in unison.

"Glad I'm here too," he says and smiles. "My name is Miller and I'm a grateful recovering alcoholic. I was born in the backwoods of Georgia—the seventh of seven children. I had three older brothers and an older sister. One Sunday morning, my mama had a stroke and died while playing the piano at church. I was four-years-old. My daddy did the best he could raising me, but losing Mama shook him up. My older brothers had joined the service, so it was left up to my big sister, Myrna, to raise me. She spoiled me rotten, letting me run wild all over Baker County. I started smoking cigarettes at thirteen. At fourteen I started drinking corn whiskey—and I loved it. It made me feel stronger, smarter, and better-looking." A couple of people chuckle.

"In ninth grade, I dropped out of school. Did odd jobs. Built fences. Worked in the corn fields, picked tomatoes and cucumbers and tried to keep those Georgia gnats from gnawing off my face."

There's a round of laughter. Daddy halfway smiles.

"Mostly I ran around with my buddies, drinking, smoking, chasing girls. My sister said I could charm the devil out of his pitchfork. By seventeen, I had worn out my welcome, so I joined the Navy to get out of Georgia. Liquor was cheap and easy to get in the service. Then one day, I was on a Greyhound bus going back to the base in Charleston and I saw a brunette dressed in a red skirt and a white blouse. I introduced myself. She was friendly, but shy. A real proper lady. Best-looking woman I had ever laid my eyes on."

"A few months later, I got down on my knees and asked her if she loved me enough to marry me. She said she did. Her mother said I was trouble with capital *T*, but we got married anyway. A year later when she went into labor, a neighbor had to drive her to the hospital. I showed up drunk the next day. And I continued to drink. My wife did not like the way I was living. She wanted our child to be raised right.

"After I got out of the Navy, I got a job in the cotton mill and found some friends who loved to drink as much as I did. And I did what I pleased. Never lifted a finger to help my wife around the house. Six years later, our second daughter was born, and for a while, I managed to stay sober. I attended church regularly, but within a year, I started drinking again.

"And I kept doing *exactly* what I wanted to do. Fishing—playing basketball—bowling. Wrecked a few cars. Had my license revoked a few times. Co-signed a loan for a friend and forged my wife's signature. That friend skipped town. Many nights, I came home stumbling drunk," he pauses, takes another sip of water.

"My wife was worn out and depressed. We both worked six days a week. Our oldest daughter took care of our youngest daughter. I criticized how they looked, what they said, and how they acted. Many times I tried to stop drinking, but I was a hopeless, pathetic drunk."

"A few years later, we had twin boys. I hung out with bigger liars and drunker drunks. Our oldest daughter got married to get out of the house. Our youngest daughter acted like I was invisible. Another family took her under their wing. I was worthless as a husband, as a father, and as a man.

"Three years ago, I went to the hospital with a bad case of pneumonia. After a day or two of not drinking, I went through delirium tremens and escaped from the hospital in a snowstorm with a pair of scissors. They found me shivering in the bushes, cutting holly berries off the trees. They put me in a straitjacket. Took me to the psychiatric ward. Or at least that's what they told me. I don't remember any of it. After that, I went to the Veteran's Hospital to sober up and finally ended up at Winding Springs where I realized that alcohol had completely taken over my life—and had also kept me acting like a teenager my whole life.

"When I got home, I went to AA meetings, worked the steps, and slowly—day by day—I became a decent husband and father. I also began to help other alcoholics, bringing them to meetings and helping them find jobs. In a few months," he says, face radiant. "I will become a grandfather for the first time.

"Now, I need to tell you how I came to be in this fellowship. One day, I was fishing with a friend of mine. We were high as kites on Southern Comfort. My friend looked at me, shook his head, and said that beside himself, I was the sorriest father he'd ever met. He said I ought to quit bragging on my young'uns all the time—and quit talking about how much I loved my wife—I did not even deserve *to have a family*. Said if I kept drinking with him, I would lose them. Then he handed me the phone number of a friend who was in AA." Daddy pulls the slip of paper from his wallet and holds it the air, looking halfway devastated. I wonder which drinking buddy he's talking about.

"The next day, I dialed the number and attended my first AA meeting that night. But my friend was not lucky like me. He never attended a meeting and never stopped drinking. And last year, he died in a terrible tragedy." Daddy pauses and pinches the bridge of his nose to squelch his tears. The room is quiet as a morgue.

Finally, he lifts his head and surveys the room. "If my friend had not given me that phone number, I would not be standing here. My family would be visiting me in a psychiatric ward, a prison, or the cemetery. Thanks for letting me share my story."

Members call out in unison, *Thanks for sharing* and applaud.

I think about Crawdad Jenkins. I never had a kind thought about that man. Never made a decent gesture toward him. I don't even know how he got that terrible nickname. But I know he was crazy enough to kill owls and eat flaming marshmallows right off the stick. And bewildered enough to kill the most wonderful boy I have ever known.

He was also the man who helped save my daddy's life.

PART IV

Be Ye Not Stiff-necked

Damsel, I say unto thee, arise.
Mark 5:41

CHAPTER 37

Don't Hardly Get on her Nerves

March 27, 1972

Dear Captain Mathilda,

I love this old crumbled down rock house. Lavender phlox creeping up the side. Dogwoods lifting their blood-tinged crosses toward the blue sky. Walking along the pebbled path that leads to the egg shaped pond. My great aunt lugged the rocks to build this place. I came to Sadie's Pond to live deliberately. To watch the sun rise and set every day. To walk around in the woods. Most of all—I came here to drive life into a corner—and reduce it to its lowest terms—so I could get the whole and genuine meanness of it like Henry David Thoreau endeavored to do at Walden.

Mama wasn't happy when I told her I was going to stay at Sadie's Pond during spring break for a little stretch of solitude. Ever since your house sold in January, I haven't had a place to think my own thoughts. So I asked Wendell to help me fix up Sadie's shack. It's a cute little cottage now with everything a person would need—a sink, a toilet, a two-burner hot plate, a single bed, and a small round table. Wendell has turned out to be a decent husband, son-in-law, and brother-in-law.

He also taught Mama how to drive, and after all these years, she finally got her license. Last night, she drove out here and brought some of her golden-crusted cornbread, black-eyed peas, and tart juicy coleslaw. We sat out by the pond, and all she talked about was the English class she's taking in night school. She raved about what a good teacher Mrs. Helms is! I told her I thought she was a good teacher too—once we got over that kerfuffle about the pronunciation of hierarchy in the school spelling bee.

Regarding the Native Daughter Scholarship, I know it is a wonderful opportunity. And I know I need to get out of Red Clover. I feel like I'm walking around in the Billy Ray Jenkins' Museum and House of Cracked Mirrors. The best tribute I can make to Billy Ray is to become a human dynamo like Marie Beynon Ray wrote about in that book you gave me. My goal is to muster up enough energy and strength to live TWO LIFETIMES IN ONE—my life and Billy Ray's—which is a better solution than diving into the deep end of Sadie's Pond with my arms tied. Somebody has to be happy in this world. Why not Karlene Kaye Bridges? I cannot let the sadness from my past gobble up my future.

I also got inspired after reading Angelina Grimké's journal about that rip-roaring speech she gave on May 17, 1838. It was the first speech in the United States ever made by a white woman to an audience of both men and women. Angelina was in the middle of her speech when an anti-abolitionist mob surrounded Pennsylvania Hall, but she was unfazed by rocks shattering the windows. She whipped up an impromptu response. She said so what if the mob burst open the doors, broke up their meeting, and assaulted them. It wouldn't be anything compared to what the slaves had to endure. Must have been heartbreaking for Angelina to see the mob burn that brand new building to the ground. And to experience the same kind of hatred in the North as she had in the South.

I am eager to see you and to meet Dr. Oglethorpe next month. I can't wait to see Hair, the Musical. My English teacher, said it was invigorating. Hugs and kisses to the gang.

Yours in perpetuity,
Karlene the Conqueror

It's cool outside, so I put on my fringed jacket and walk toward the pond noticing the fluffy white clouds strewn across the bright blue sky, remembering all the good times Billy Ray and I had here. I loved watching that boy fish—he always looked as if he were praying. But he also had that teasing sense of humor—which got on my nerves. These days, he hardly ever gets on my nerves. The cornpone girl inside of me takes that thought and spouts lyrics:

> *Billy Ray don't hardly get on my nerves, si-ince he died—*
> *but my heartstrings are still tied up in one great big knot—*
> *that I've been trying to unravel—one tear at a time—*
> *but God knows there's plenty more—where those tears came from.*

A tune blows across the lyrics like a hot breeze, and the music and words twine into a song. I belt it out in that swing-low, sweet chariot, coming-for-to-carry-me home voice that shows how I feel about being left on this earth without Billy Ray. My favorite part is that *God knows* expression at the end. Mama says it's like taking the Lord's name in vain, but it honors the fact that sometimes, life is a vale of tears.

CHAPTER 38

Explicitness of His Savior

I gaze out at the hundred or so members of Free Will Pentecostal Holiness Church, who built this white cinderblock sanctuary and the pews on which they sit. Billy Ray's mama sits on the front row beside her daddy, Pastor Richards, who just introduced me. Mama and Daddy sit on the second row, their hands clutched together as if they're afraid of what I might say. Kelly sits on the back row between Noah and Joshua—and gives me a big thumbs up.

"Thanks Pastor Richards, for inviting me to speak today. Last night, I felt terrified, but now that I'm standing here, I feel joyous because I am here to honor my best friend, Billy Ray Jenkins—a young man whose presence is felt in this church today. A young man who could explain electrons and valences and formulas and isotopes like a scientist—and who knew the Periodic Table by heart. Billy Ray and I had the same lunch period. One day, I was in a foul mood but Billy Ray ignored it and told me about the elements that had been discovered since he was born: *nobelium, lawrencium, rutherfordium, and dubnium.* And he said if *he* ever discovered an element, he'd name it *karlenium.* That's just how clever and sassy he was."

I pause for a moment, then lift Billy Ray's red Bible and hold it in the air. "How many remember the summer Billy Ray carried around this Bible given to him by his granddaddy, your very own Pastor

Richards?" Fifteen or so hands go up, including the Pastor, whose eyes light up at the mention of his gift.

"The first time I saw Billy Ray carrying it, we were on a camping trip, so I just hauled off and asked: Don't all those *woes, begats* and *verilys* get on your nerves? He said no, he liked them just fine. Then I asked: What about all those *hateths, loveths,* and *obeyeths?* Billy Ray said those "eths" at the end made the words sound *kinder*," I say, rolling my eyes. "That boy always had the last word when it came to scripture."

Kelly grins on the back row. Even Teeny cracks a smile.

"And for the rest of the summer, Billy Ray bored me to pieces talking about the Gospel of Matthew. So when Mrs. Jenkins asked me to speak for Youth Sunday, I began to study the Book of Matthew and realized why Billy Ray was so impressed. Jesus did not pussyfoot around. The first sentence Jesus speaks in the New Testament is: *SUFFER IT TO BE SO NOW.*" I pause, letting the sentence resonate in the sanctuary.

"Jesus spoke those six words to John the Baptist because John was reluctant to baptize Jesus because he did not feel worthy of the task. But Jesus told him he must bear his feelings of unworthiness—and baptize him anyway. Billy Ray Jenkins followed Jesus's *Suffer it to be so now* commandment. He chose to bear up to any difficulty he encountered—never making excuses.

"We need to keep that commandment close to our hearts to remind ourselves we are capable of bearing up to our troubles— whether it's the death of a loved one—or maybe we cannot forgive ourselves for something we did or did not do. We need to offer up those things to something greater than ourselves," I say, suddenly struck by the beauty and simplicity of what it means.

"The second time Jesus speaks in Matthew, he's lonely, tired and hungry because he's been fasting and praying in the wilderness for forty days. He's confused, doubting, trying to offer up his whole life to God. And that's exactly when Satan shows up—because he smells Jesus's weakness. But Jesus rebukes Satan: *Get thee Hence, Satan.* He doesn't *ask* Satan to go away—He demands it.

"In the next Chapter, when Jesus delivers the Sermon on the Mount, he does *not* warm up the crowd by telling a cute joke. He starts out telling them EXACTLY who the BLESSED are. The poor in spirit, those that mourn, those that hunger and thirst after righteousness, the merciful, the pure in heart, the peacemakers, and those persecuted for righteousness sake. He says to REJOICE and let our light SHINE. To pluck out our offending eyes. And to NEVER swear—which is harder for some of us than others," I say, looking at Mama in supplication.

"Jesus then gives *explicit* instructions on how to pray. Do NOT repeat other people's prayers. Do NOT grandstand in public. Shut out the world—and find a closet to pray in. Then He tells them EXACTLY what to pray when he gives them the Lord's Prayer—which is a very fine prayer—but it's also ironic because he just told them NOT to repeat other people's prayers.

"Next, Jesus gets down to the real nitty-gritty—telling us how to be whole: 1) Love God with our hearts, souls, and minds. 2) Love our neighbors as ourselves. 3) Go out into the world and behave ourselves. 4) Get baptized, which as we learned, even Jesus did. 5) Teach everyone how they are supposed to behave. Which is what I'm doing now," I say, feeling ecstatic because I know Billy Ray would love how I said it in a lighthearted way.

"My goal today was to deliver the gospel in a way that would have pleased Billy Ray. He thought it was better to let his life speak for itself than to rattle off a sermon that might go off course at any moment without him even knowing it—like mine has done several times this morning.

"Mrs. Jenkins and Pastor Richards, my heart goes out to you today as we remember Billy Ray on what would have been his twenty-first birthday. I'd like to close with Billy Ray's favorite verse: Matthew 6: 22, *The light of the body is the eye: if therefore thine eye be single, thy whole body shall be full of light.* Billy Ray's eye was singular. He believed that everything he did was his Maker's business. Guess that's why his whole body was full of light. He dearly loved both of you, and he tried his very best," I say, searching for what Billy Ray *most wanted to be,* and the answer pours out like purifying rain, "to be a good son."

CHAPTER 39

She pushed and she pushed

On the first day of April, late afternoon sunlight streams through the tall, skinny windows of the library onto my overly pregnant sister lounging in a comfy chair with a parenting magazine. I sit at a long oak table and open *The Complete Book of Breast-feeding* that has 432 pages, which seems ridiculously long for something that is one hundred percent natural. It took Gloria Jean two weeks to read it, but she said it was fascinating. I'll read the first paragraph before Miss Sophia shelves it.

> *If you were living at some other time or in some other place, you might not need this book. You might even wonder about its purpose, since you would be getting much of the information of these pages from your mother, your aunts, your older sister, and your neighbors. They would share with you their breast-feeding experiences and those of their mothers before them. As you saw them suckling their infants, you would pick up the "tricks of the trade" without even realizing it. It would never occur to you that you would not nurse your baby, because every baby that you had ever seen would have been fed at his mother's breast.*

I read further and discover the authors are alarmed because only ONE out of FOUR women even *attempted* to breastfeed their babies last year—the lowest rate in U.S. history. Sounds as if humans are trying to divorce ourselves from the Mammal Kingdom.

"Baby just kicked a field goal!" Gloria Jean says.

"Are you all right?" I ask.

"Yes, but I need a milkshake." She hoists herself from the chair.

"I'll take you to the Jiffy Grill." I mosey to the circulation desk.

"Just two today?" Miss Sophia says, stamping the date on *I'm O.K, You're O.K.*—but when she sees *Deliverance* by James Dickey, a professor at the University of South Carolina, she stares at me with big owly eyes. "This is the most unedifying book ever written by a Southerner—it's not appropriate for—"

"Oh Lordy!" Gloria Jean hollers, standing in a puddle of water.

Fifteen minutes later, Wendell, Gloria Jean, and I storm into Doc Smith's office. Nurse Becky puts her arm around Gloria Jean. "How you feeling, Honey?"

"Hunky-dory," Gloria Jean says, trying to act all confident.

Nurse Becky raises her eyebrows. "Scared as hell?"

Gloria Jean smiles sheepishly.

Doc Smith strolls in. "Let's take a look," he says, then leads her to the examination room.

Wendell waits in the reception area with me, pacing back and forth. I sit in a squeaky chair, worrying about how that big baby is going to get out of my tiny sister. The five o'clock L & N train rumbles down the tracks—whistling its going-someplace-else song. I remember how Billy Ray loved that sound, and a tingling sensation comes over me. Maybe Billy Ray's soul *is* on that train, and it's blowing the whistle to let me know a new soul's about to come into this world through my sister. Maybe it could even be Billy Ray's soul reincarnated.

Finally, the doctor comes out. "You have plenty of time to get her to the hospital. She has only dilated 3.5 centimeters. "

"Doc, I'm lousy at the metric system. How many inches is that?"

"About 1.5 inches," he says.

"What is the average circumference of a baby's head?"

"Oh, about 14 inches or so."

Poor Gloria Jean has a lot more stretching to do.

Doc tells us to go ahead. He'll come to the hospital later.

Wendell sits in the back seat, comforting Gloria Jean as I drive his shiny blue Lincoln north on Main Street. Mama Cass belts out that song on the radio about how I need to make my own kind of music—and sing my own special song—even if no one else in the world cares to hear me sing it. I turn into the parking lot of High Memorial Hospital, the new improved version of the hospital I was born in—where Daddy had the DTs—and Mama had her hysterectomy last year.

Mama and Daddy are already waiting in the lobby. Wendell, Mama, and I take shifts staying with Gloria Jean, feeding her slivers of ice, and putting a cold cloth on her forehead. Daddy doesn't know what to do, so he just goes around visiting sick people he doesn't even know, trying to stay out of the way. The cruelest part is how slowly the minute hand twitches around the huge round clock on the wall.

At ten o'clock that night, labor pains push through Gloria Jean like a train bursting out the side of a mountain. You can tell she feels like cussing, but screams *Yikes* instead. By midnight, we've heard a thousand yikes. And Gloria Jean doesn't care if the whole world sees her bottom. *Will some body pull this baby out of me?* I feel so sorry for her as they wheel her to the delivery room.

I mosey down to the cafeteria for a cup of coffee and sit over by the window. I pull out Spencer's most recent letter and reread the part about how sexy I smell, how delicious and delectable I taste, and what a genuinely sweet girl I am, which sounds ridiculous, especially the being sweet part. Spencer is the sexy-smelling one. And a suave slow dancer. And he's passionate as they come. Lord, do I miss that man. To distract myself, I pull a sheet of paper and a pen from my book satchel and start writing:

Dear Spencer,

Here I sit in the cafeteria of High Springs Memorial Hospital feeling sorry for myself because I miss your face—and other parts of you as well. Meanwhile in the delivery room, Gloria Jean yells out one yikes after another. That's how self-absorbed I am. When it comes to love, I am greedy as a little rat. My most acute sense is touch, and to tell you the truth, I feel I have a deficit in the being touched department. Touching or being touched by someone can be a very special way to communicate.

When you held my face so tenderly in your hands and said you were completely upside over me, I did not say anything, but I felt like I was in some kind of upside down, mystical love spiral. I truly appreciate how you take me and my body seriously. You even take my silly songs seriously. Thanks for sending me the latest version of "The High Road." I love what you said about how songs are meant to lift people out of themselves into another dimension of space and time—and how songs don't need to be perfect—they just need to be gen-u-wine. "The High Road" fits that description perfectly. It made me think about the literal and metaphorical roads I've been down, and the ones I anticipate like seeing you again—and the ones I dread like if you end up in Vietnam. And I truly loved that part about how if you stay on the high road long enough—your heart will turn to gold. It felt authentic to me—not the cliché you feared.

Consider yourself touched in all the right places,
Karlene, the soon-to-be-Aunt

p.s. Yesterday, I tried to play my harmonica with one hand and beat the tambourine against my leg with the other. Blew my fuses— like trying to pat my head and rub my tummy. Might work if I had a neck rack for the harmonica and two hands free for the tambourine.

I stop there—keeping it zippy and real and upbeat. No use to mention how he's been transferred to Fairchild Air Force Base and is right now taking a survival course on how *not* to get captured and what to do if he *does* get captured. Or how I found out that doing search and rescue is especially hazardous to a crewman's life. I say a quick prayer for Spencer Randall and his buddies and pray for my sister to remain healthy and whole and to deliver a spectacular baby girl. Then I grab my satchel and head to the waiting room.

It's two o'clock in the morning when Gloria Jean wakes in a regular room. I'm standing against the wall. Mama's sitting on the bed, telling Gloria Jean she lost a lot of blood, and that Doc Smith had to do a lot of repair work down there. Sluggish and a little bit weepy, Gloria Jean says all she remembers is how bright the lights were in the delivery room and how Doc Smith sat between her legs urging her to push and push and push—and she must have passed out after that.

"When can I see my baby?"

"Soon," Mama says.

"Where's my knight in shining armor?" she asks with no sarcasm whatsoever.

"Wendell went to buy cigars," Mama says.

I hand Gloria Jean a glass of water. "How do you feel?"

"Like my bottom's been turned inside out, burned with a torch, and blasted by a fire extinguisher." She lifts the sheet and looks at her baby-less belly. "Who in the world put this giant Kotex and sanitary belt on me?"

"It wasn't me," Wendell says as he walks into the room and kisses her forehead, his lips lingering for a few seconds. He stands back, full of pride. "That's some baby we made—pretty doesn't begin to cover it."

"Honey, please make them bring her to me," Gloria Jean says.

Wendell goes to find the nurse, and a few minutes later, a skinny, fiftyish, redheaded nurse comes into the room carrying a bundle wrapped in a pink flannel blanket. Gloria Jean opens her arms. The nurse hands the baby to her, acting almost haughty, as if she thinks Gloria Jean doesn't know how to care for a baby. But when Gloria Jean holds her seven-pound baby girl to her breast, the baby roots around trying to find her mama's nipple. Wendell can't take his eyes off his two girls. Gloria Jean smiles at him. She doesn't care that breast-feeding has gone out of style. She wants the best nourishment for her baby.

As the baby nuzzles against Gloria Jean's breast, I worry that my niece will have that dreamy, wonder-why-I-am-here kind of feeling I've had almost every day of my life. If so—she's going to need a gutsy sounding name to make her feel like she belongs on this earth. Something distinctive like Lila Mae, Gloria Jean or Karlene Kaye.

"What are you going to name her?" I say.

"I love the name Jessie," Wendell says. "Jessie sounds like somebody with gumption."

"Sounds like a gunslinger," Gloria Jean says. "But I like it."

I like it too. And suddenly, the word *joy* pops into my mind.

"How about Jessie Joy—baby girl of Gloria Jean and Wendell?"

"Jessie Joy sounds perfect to me," Mama says.

"Sounds perfect to me too," Gloria Jean squeals.

Wendell grins. "Okay Aunt Karlene, Jessie Joy Whetstone it is."

CHAPTER 40

Promises of the Promised Land

A few days after Jessie Joy came into this world, I take a soul-restoring bath, put on my pajamas and go to my room to watch a special program about Martin Luther King that Ms. Flowers assigned us to watch. We listened to parts of his Memphis speech in class today. I turn on my little black and white TV, slip between the covers and relax as the show begins with a CBS newsreel from April 1968 with a close-up of President Johnson's hound-dog face announcing the assassination of the "apostle of nonviolence."

Then they cut to Senator Bobby Kennedy on the campaign trail in California as he breaks the bad news about Reverend King's death. He tells the crowd that his heart had almost been poisoned by hatred when his brother was assassinated, but he dug deep inside himself and found compassion. I feel bad for poor Bobby. He has no idea his name will be erased in the Book of Life in a couple of months.

Next, they show an excerpt of Dr. King giving his speech in Memphis the day before he died. He starts by taking the audience on an imaginary tour of his life, saying that God Almighty called him by name and asked him which age he wanted to live in. Instead of answering, the Reverend soars off like an eagle through time. He flies by Egypt, across the Red Sea, toward the Promised Land, but doesn't stop there. He flies to Mount Olympus to see Plato, Aristotle and Socrates discussing the eternal issues but doesn't stop there. He soars to the heyday of the Roman Empire but doesn't stop there. He observes the Renaissance but doesn't stop there. He flies onward through time and sees his namesake, Martin Luther, as he tacks his ninety-five theses on the church door, but he doesn't stop there. He stops in 1863 to see Abraham Lincoln sign the Emancipation Proclamation, but he doesn't stop there. He flies to the Great Depression and hears the FDR cry out: *We have nothing to fear but fear itself.*

That's when Dr. King comes to a screeching halt and asks the Almighty to let him live for a few years in the second half of the twentieth century because our nation is in turmoil. Then Dr. King really gets to preaching. He exhorts his people to rise up and shout for freedom. To stop scratching where they don't itch. To stop laughing when it ain't funny. To keep marching until they get what is rightfully theirs. He tells them not to buy Coca-Cola, Sealtest Milk, or Wonder Bread until Memphis treats the sanitation workers right. *Nothing* would be more tragic than for them to stop their fight, he says, his voice warbly as an old man's. My nerves are shot, so I turn off the television and lie on my bed.

Dr. King's words swirl around inside me.

The passion in his voice makes me think he was *born to make that speech.* Maybe he was *born to die the next day.* I think about him standing on that hotel balcony in Memphis joshing around with his friends before supper, when bang—a bullet takes his life away. That verse from Hebrews floats into my head. *It is a terrible thing to fall into the hands of the living God. .*

Maybe Dr. King had such an intense relationship with his Maker, there wasn't any wiggle room to ignore God's will. Maybe after spending thirty-nine years in the hands of the living God, he was itching to put his feet up and sip lemonade for an eternity or two. Maybe he *knew* Memphis was the last door of his life.

I think about the questions Ms. Flowers asked us to reflect upon while watching the program: *Where did Dr. King's POWER come from? How did he use it? What benefits did he get from it?*

The answers are all in his speech in Memphis.

Dr. King's power came from the Almighty, which he channeled into speeches and sermons that changed people's hearts and minds and helped them understand we were bound together in a single garment of destiny. And because of his faith, Martin wasn't worried about anything. The Almighty even empowered him to give his own eulogy in Memphis. Dr. King had already been to the mountaintop and seen the promised land—it did not matter if *he* reached it—he knew people would get there no matter what.

I think about how Billy Ray grew up hearing his granddaddy preach every Sunday just like Martin heard his daddy preach. Billy Ray also had an intense relationship with his Maker and didn't give himself much wiggle room either. Being in the hands of the living God might have worn him out. I remember how distracted and depressed he was when we sat on the porch steps the last time I saw him. Perhaps he knew what lay behind the door to his Daddy's trailer and felt he had no choice but to open it.

CHAPTER 41

Life ain't a dirty chore

A tall, slender, athletically built woman with short, stylish silver hair extends her slender hand and shakes mine, directing me to an overstuffed purple love seat. Then she sits in a matching chair across from me with a notebook in her lap. "Hello, Karlene, I am delighted to finally meet you."

"Thanks, Dr. Oglethorpe, I am delighted to meet you."

"What did you think of the tour of our campus?"

"The architecture is grand, the landscaping lovely, and that library is out of this world."

"Tell me, have you thought of a topic you'd like to pursue during your first year at Smith College—that is, if you are selected for the Native Daughter scholarship?"

"I'm still terribly interested in the topic of human sexuality, the empowerment of women, and the role of literature like I wrote about in my essay comparing the fictional lives of Emma Bovary, Anna Karenina, and Tess to the real lives of Sarah and Angelina Grimké."

"But why is this topic so important to *you* in particular?"

"This human sexuality business has always made me feel like a big dumb isosceles triangle, but I read a book a while ago that opened my eyes. It's called *How Never to Be Tired.* The author, Marie Beynon Ray had tremendous insights about human sexuality. She said human beings had two primary drives in their subconscious minds. The SEX URGE and the DESIRE TO BE IMPORTANT."

Her eyebrows form into little teepees. "Please tell me more."

"She said that every person needs to find work that makes them feel important and they also need to find a way to satisfy their sexual desires. If *either* of these urges is thwarted for too long, life itself begins to feel like some kind of dirty chore."

"Life as a dirty chore. Such original phrasing."

"Thank you, ma'am. It's part of a song that's been floating around in my head for a while about how funny we look, running around without a clue about what we're supposed to do in this world. I titled it "Lord Have Mercy on Us All.""

"Mind singing a bit of it for me?"

"Don't mind at all—I'll sing the first stanza."

> *Don't you hurry no more*
> *life ain't a dirty chore*
> *to get done quickly as you can*
> *before you even understand*
> *that everything you do*
> *comes back around*
> *and slaps or kisses you.*

"Your song has a country twang," she says, eyes sparkling.

"Pardon me, ma'am. My songs just come out the way they come out."

"No pardon necessary—even Bob Dylan went to Nashville and recorded an album."

"*Nashville Skyline* is one of my favorites," I say, thrilled to be simpatico.

She smiles warmly. "What else did the author have to say about human sexuality?"

"In Europe, when a boy or girl becomes neurotic due to their sexual urges being stifled—psychiatrists often advise them *to get a sweetheart and have sex relations*. But the author said that was like turning love and marriage into some kind of perfunctory medicine, which shortchanges young people. She thinks Dr. Adler—whoever he is—has the right idea: YOUNG PEOPLE SHOULD CHOOSE THEIR LIFE'S WORK AS EARLY AS POSSIBLE. That way, they can pour their primal impulses into their work—sparing them the agony of sexual frustration."

"Hold on," she says, her pen flying across the page of her notebook.

Damn. I should have kept my big mouth shut. Probably ruined the whole interview. I visualize positive adjectives flowing from Dr. Oglethorpe's pen: PROFOUND, ASTUTE, PERCEPTIVE, BRILLIANT, ARTICULATE, PROGRESSIVE—then words like OUTRAGEOUS, BEWILDERED, DERANGED and SEXUALLY FRUSTRATED. I hope to God I haven't offended her. Dr. Oglethorpe quits writing and looks at me as if she's delighted. "I am glad you mentioned Dr. Alfred Adler, who was a brilliant psychotherapist and psychologist. My theory of education is built on his tenet that educators must believe in the potential power of their pupils and do everything possible to help their students realize their own power."

"Wow," I say, "That sounds just like my English teacher's theory. Power has been a big topic in our class this year. We discuss how it manifests in our own lives and in literature. I've learned more in Ms. Flower's class than any class in high school."

"Your teacher sounds exceptional, but let's get back to our topic. What qualifies *you* to tackle such a monumental issue as human sexuality?"

I pause for a moment, letting the words *tackle, monumental,* and *sexuality* coalesce in my mind. "Besides exploring my own sexuality, I have also done tons of research on the topic, but more importantly, my spirit has not been contaminated by our patriarchal system. We need to move away from the male centric model of sexuality and embrace female sexuality. We are conditioned beings, ma'am. We do as others did before us, good or bad. My goal is to break the ties that bind me to unintelligent thought and behavior."

"I have even found references in the Bible that embolden me, such as: *Be ye not stiff-necked, as your fathers were—and be ye not conformed to this world: but be ye transformed by the renewing of your mind.* That's why I want to come to Smith College, Dr. Oglethorpe. I want to focus on women's issues. I want to inspire other young women to acknowledge and celebrate our bodies, mind, and spirit. I want to help stamp out ignorance about female sexuality."

We just sit there quietly, absorbing each other's energy.

"How would you go about addressing this ignorance?"

"First, all children should be taught the proper names for our body parts and how they function. We have perfectly good words to describe our anatomy. We need to use them. Otherwise, the human body turns into some kind of dirty joke. Second, we need to make the study of human emotion as important as the study of the alphabet. There's some serious ignorance in this world about our FEELINGS. I guess that's why I became a bookworm at such a young age—to understand the inner workings of people's hearts and minds. Literature helps me understand our emotions. The finer ones such as love and respect, and the coarser ones such as lust and greed. Perhaps if we understood our feelings, we could communicate them—instead of walking around lonely and confused half the time. Trust me, Dr. Oglethorpe, that's no way to live."

"Karlene, you have brought up some excellent points about educating ourselves about emotions and using the right vocabulary for our anatomy. You've also discussed men's attitudes about women. What about women's attitudes toward other women? Aren't we misogynists? Haven't we been taught to blame Eve and to hate ourselves for almost everything from the very beginning?"

"I've never really thought that much about women hating ourselves and each other. But my mother told me the story about when she announced her first pregnancy to her mother, her mother just flat out insulted her—saying Mama didn't have enough sense to raise a baby. I don't know what made her say such a hateful thing. Maybe it's because bringing a child into this world is such a huge responsibility—and my father wasn't the most reliable husband at the time."

Dr. Oglethorpe points to a poster on the wall of Virginia Woolf. "What do you think of her epigram?"

I study the words: *Arrange whatever pieces come your way.*

That six word imperative sentence wallops my brain.

"Who else is there to arrange the piece of our lives?" I reply.

She smiles, intrigued by my answer, so I continue.

"Women are particularly good at arranging the pieces of their lives. In fact, they excel in the everydayness of life. My mother is a perfect example. She takes care of our home, our family, and herself. She has worked at High Cotton Mills for 20 years. She pays taxes and tithes 10% of her income to the church. She has raised four children to the best of her ability. She has been a supportive wife during my father's alcoholism and his treatment. She helps other women whose husbands have the same problem. Another great example is Mrs. Harrison, who enticed me to apply for this scholarship, as you know. She is a brilliant educator, a fine mother, a devoted wife, and a divine human being. Without her, I would not be the happy scholar I am today."

"Touché," she says, with laughing eyes. "Tell me, Karlene, where do you see yourself in fifteen years?"

"In the Governor's office, leading South Carolina out of its ignorance," I say as if I were a deadly serious gubernatorial candidate.

"Let me do the math," she says, figuring in her head. "So you plan to become governor of South Carolina by the time you are thirty-three-years old?"

"To be honest ma'am—I have never imagined myself as staying in South Carolina long enough to become governor."

"Suppose you *were* the governor. How would you lead South Carolina out of its so-called ignorance?"

Damn it all to hell. My eager beaverness could wreck the entire interview. I force myself to relax and pray for an elegant solution. After a few rounds of breathing, Step Four surfaces in the eight ball in my mind: *Made a searching and fearless moral inventory of ourselves.*

"Well, ma'am, the first thing I would do is to conduct a searching and fearless moral inventory of South Carolina's current policies and past deeds. This inventory would have to be a top-secret project conducted by a small group of historians and lofty thinkers—otherwise, people would think I was a lunatic. But after a thorough analysis, I'd know exactly what amends were needed—and I'd do everything in my power to put South Carolina on the road to recovery. And I'd probably start by erecting a large memorial to the Grimké Sisters for their heroic campaign for women's suffrage and the abolition of slavery."

"Sounds downright utopian," she says in a friendly voice that lets me know the hard part of the interview is over. "Beside the governorship, what other jobs interest you?"

"When I was little, I wanted to become a doctor and move to Africa like Dr. Schweitzer. I've even thought about going to Hollywood to write some decent, sexy love stories after watching *Carnal Knowledge* and getting creeped out by it. And since my friend Billy Ray died, I've even considered going into the ministry. But I doubt there's a church in the United States of America that would want me as their pastor."

"There are all kinds of pulpits out there you don't even know about," she says, cocking her head. "Pulpits *and* battlefields—and I think you'd be welcome in quite a few."

"Thank you, ma'am. That word battlefield brings up another topic that interests me. My friend Spencer joined the Air Force last year, thinking the worst of the war was over, but now, he and and his buddies are dropping bombs all over North Vietnam. If peace is ever going to be made, Dr. Oglethorpe, I believe women will have to make it. War is second nature to men, especially the generals. The poor soldiers who have to fight end up with their souls damaged, and they wander around not having a clue about what to do with their lives. Perhaps it's time for women to get together and establish the *United States Peace College* to study peace around the clock since the U. S. Army established the War College back in 1901 to study war around the clock."

"Excellent idea. I sure would love to hear what your mother thinks about your diverse ambitions."

"She would probably prefer I get the governor's job or become a doctor."

"It's refreshing to meet an intelligent young woman who speaks with candor." She stands and extends her hand.

I stand and shake her hand firmly. "I believe women hold the key to human progress. We need to work hard on the issues, but we also need to lighten up on ourselves. That's why I want to come to Smith College—to focus on the empowerment and jollification of women."

"Our committee meets later today. We have the Harrison's phone number. We'll call you." She escorts me to the reception area, and Mrs. Harrison walks up grinning like a court jester. She and Dr. Oglethorpe start chitchatting like long lost friends.

I walk outside, look up into the vast blue Connecticut sky, and pray to God I just finagled a ticket out of Red Clover.

CHAPTER 42

Whole lot of soul

It's after midnight when Mrs. Harrison and I step out of the taxi and find ourselves standing in Times Square. Holy Damn Moly! I turn 360 degrees like a human carousel. The hustle and bustle vibrates through every layer of my skin, connecting me to all these beating hearts, sky-high buildings, and flashing neon lights. People hollering—laughing—celebrating. And for the second time in my life, I stand in New York City beside the amazing Amanda Mathilda Harrison. Buses whiz by. Taxis honk. Women in miniskirts skitter along the sidewalk in spiky heeled shoes. And my mind whirls with the salty lyrics, naked bodies, and all that gleaming, steaming, flaxen, long beautiful hair from *Hair!* A headline flashes in my mind: *Happy Scholarship Winner from South Carolina Spontaneously Combusts After Seeing Mind-Blowing Musical.*

Thank God we got the news when we got back to the Harrisons' apartment. Now, Captain Mathilda stands three feet away, her head cocked with I-told-you-so written all over her face. She starts singing Little Eva's song about how everybody's doing a brand new dance and for me to come on and do it with her. She shakes her butt and sings how it's easy as learning our ABCs—even her little baby sister can do it. She makes chooga-chooga motions with her arms. Nice and easy with a whole lot of soul. I wrap my arms around her waist and we locomote down the sidewalk, swerving in and out of the crowd. A few people stop and watch our show. Captain Mathilda hams it up big time, and I follow as if we're in our own private musical. And I don't give a flip if anyone thinks I'm the least bit silly. I *am* silly.

And I am exactly where I want to be.

My mojo rising to the occasion.

CHAPTER 43

A Tramp Shining

Around eleven o'clock, the night before graduation, I look at the pictures on my bedroom wall. Aretha wearing a glittery turquoise dress, her lips touching a big shiny microphone. Ringo, with a goofy grin and that big purple heart I colored on his chest. He looks out of place, perched beside the *Graveyard of Recently Departed Rock Stars* that's decorated with the *Rolling Stone* covers of Janis Joplin, Jimi Hendrix, and Jim Morrison. Might as well start dismantling my life now.

The Queen of Soul comes off first. I roll up the poster and put a rubber band around it. Aretha is such good company—I'll take her with me. Ringo's going with me, too. He's still the most under-appreciated of the former Beatles, but he's doing fine with "It Don't Come Easy," that respectable hit he had last year. Plus he and Maureen have a new baby. I pack Ringo and Aretha in the bottom of the new steamer trunk I bought to take to college and then bury Janis, Jimi, and Jim in the trashcan.

I need to select music to take with me. I walk to the record shelf and pull out the first album Billy Ray gave me. It's by Richard Harris—the actor who played King Arthur in *Camelot* as if he *were* King Arthur. I place the record on my Zenith, and Richard starts singing in that reflective voice of his, accompanied by the string section of the orchestra. *Here I am, a tramp shining, a brand new clow-ow-*

own. There's a long pause that lasts at least fifteen-seconds—and then he sings that *"Didn't We"* song in his beseeching vibrato voice. Didn't we almost make the pieces fit, girl? Didn't he have the answer right there in his hand? Didn't we almost sing our special song? But his voice breaks, and he calls me his dancing girl, saying how much he's going to miss me after the *curtain call.* I hate that phrase—I hate endings, period.

Then before he can get to the part where we *didn't* make it to the moon, and *didn't* get the chance to make our poem rhyme, and *didn't* get to climb to wherever the hell we *would* have climbed to, if we'd had the chance, I pull the plug out of the wall and fall back onto the bed. Tears well in my eyes and trickle down the sides of my face, pooling into my ears. I tilt my head right, then left, letting the tears flow onto the pillow.

I look at Richard Harris' ruddy face on the cover—his eyes peering out into the future like a hawk. Then I notice three words written underneath his chin in fancy typescript: *A Tramp Shining.* You never think about a tramp *shining*—you think about a tramp being dusty or dirty, hitching a ride somewhere. That dream of a hobo walking toward the setting sun plays in my head. He carries a bindle with a red sack and stops in the middle of a high arching bridge. Then he looks back over his shoulder at me high up in a tower, as if saying goodbye.

Maybe Billy Ray gave me this album to remind me about the wondrous life of tramps and hobos—how they embrace the road and choose not tarry anywhere for long. And maybe the universe sent the mysterious dream before Billy Ray died to warn me of his death and to let me know we're all just hobos on a bridge, and after we die, we're just eager to get to the other side.

CHAPTER 44

Oh those lurking dreams

My heart flip-flops like a dying catfish as I stand before two hundred and eighteen of my classmates. "I have been asked to speak today because your valedictorian, Desi Sistare, sitting there with that big wolfy grin on his face, has a serious case of laryngitis. When Desi earned the honor of being the valedictorian, I was not surprised. Desi knows something about everything—and loves to share his knowledge with anyone, anytime, or anyplace. So it's highly unfortunate that he's unable to enlighten us today. But since Mr. World Book is speechless for the first time in his entire life, I, Karlene Bridges, salutatorian of the Red Clover High School Class of 1972, have a few things I'd like to offer up for your consideration," I say, stretching my arms out toward the crowd.

"A few minutes from now, when we toss our silly caps into the air, our time at this school will be OVER. No more worrying about failing geometry—or writing that essay on transcendentalism. We will NEVER be students here again. So today is the perfect opportunity to embrace all the hilarious, miraculous, and mortifying moments we've experienced here at Red Clover High School—and accept them as a part of our history. So how about a huge hip hip hooray?"

The crowd roars *hip hip hooray, hip hip hooray, hip hip hooray!*

"I do not know about you, but goodbyes are dreadful for me. I'd rather have my tonsils and adenoids removed than to say goodbye. But today, at this important milestone in our lives, saying goodbye is a necessary thing to do. Yesterday, I looked up GOODBYE in the dictionary. The word originated in the sixteenth century. It's a contraction for the phrase *God be with you* which doesn't sound dreadful at all. So now, Desi, will you please join me?"

The crowd applauds and whistles as Desi crosses the stage.

I hand him the microphone.

"Will all seniors please stand?" he says in his froggy baritone.

Desi hands me the microphone.

"Okay, people, please turn to someone near you—look that person in the eye—and say *goodbye*." I turn toward Desi, and we say our goodbyes. Thousands of *goodbyes* fill the air—some mumbled, some whispered, and some said wholeheartedly.

"Now repeat the process with two more classmates."

The buzz of their *goodbyes* gets louder.

I holler into the microphone: "That wasn't so difficult was it?"

The crowd roars *No!* I take Desi's hand and lift it high into the air. "To the graduates of Red Clover High School Class of 1972, we say *Goodbye. Farewell. Adieu. Au revoir. Ciao. Adios. Sayonara. Bon voyage. Cheers!*"

The crowd hollers and hoots, then I ask them to sit down.

"Another word of advice I'd like to offer to all the graduates: DO NOT TARRY. It's an old-fashioned word that means to prolong your farewell—to loiter—to linger—to procrastinate—to delay. Now ask yourself: Did your loved ones raise you to follow in their footsteps, or do they want you to forge your own path? Every single one of you has a dream lurking inside you," I say, eager to rush through the next part, but my throat feels clogged with emotion. I take a few sips of water and then a few deep breaths.

"Like I said, every single one of you has a dream lurking inside you. You might have forgotten yours—but I guarantee you your dream has not forgotten you. Now, I'd like to introduce a woman, whose dream did not forget her—Lila Mae Robertson Bridges—will you please stand?"

There's a hushed feeling in the air as students look around, wondering who Lila Mae is—but then, a woman rises from the royal blue sea of students in their pomp and circumstance gowns and waves her right hand high in the air.

"Hey everybody, this is Lila Bridges, my mother. For many years, she gave a weekly lecture bemoaning the fact she dropped out of high school after eleventh grade—and that our job, as her children, was to get ourselves educated. When we suggested she go back to school, she got all snippety—as if such a thing were impossible. And we just let it slide. My brother-in-law, however, does not let anything slide. He brought up the topic on a regular basis. Mama brought up one excuse after another. He crushed every one of them. The last one being that she didn't have transportation, so he found her a decent car and taught her to drive. He wasn't about to let her forget her dream. So please, join me in a round of applause for Lila Bridges and Wendell Whetstone, her tenacious son-in-law.

The crowd grows raucous as fans at a football game.

"Thanks, everybody. Now, please refer to the back cover of your program, where you will find the lyrics to the song Desi chose for the Class of 1972." I hand Desi the microphone, and he speaks in a deep hoarse voice. "Come on, LOUD AND PROUD, sing along with the Staple Singers."

The loudspeakers blast out the bluesy instrumental at the beginning of the song and Pops Staples addresses us in his preacher's voice with a long drawn-out *Ya'll*, then sings about how we should not run around in this world disrespecting people right and left. And when he gets to the chorus, we join in, singing at the top of our voices: *Respect yourself, Respect yourself, Respect yourself!*

Later that evening, I sit on our porch swing, holding Jessie Joy, who's dressed in one of my cute little hand-me-down baby dresses. I have not been around a baby since the twins were born—I forgot how amazing they are. I nudge my pinkie into her little hand. Five tiny fingers wrap around it, even though she's asleep. I look out at the sun slipping off the edge of the world. I appreciate how dependable the sun is. Showing up for work every day. Disappearing in the evening like a happy servant. But as spectacular as this sunset is, it doesn't hold a candle to Jessie Joy who's awake now—staring up at me with curious eyes, as if she's eager to know her Aunt Karlene's take on the situation.

I lean in close to her scrunched up little face and start our first conversation. "You are one lucky little creature. Your mama and daddy are decent, hardworking people who love you to pieces already. Your grandmother, the graduate, is inside making two lemon meringue pies. Your Uncle Josh and Uncle Noah are getting wrestling lessons from your daddy. Your granddaddy's napping in his squeaky recliner. Your mama is stretched out on my bed, resting a while, because she's a mother now, and that is the toughest job on earth—which is where you are, Jessie Joy Whetstone—and a big welcome to you. I am your Aunt Karlene—and I'm glad you made it all the way here—from wherever it is you came from."

I lift my niece and hold her close, her little head resting on my shoulder. She smells like fresh-baked heaven. Mama Cass's song plays in my head, so I whisper the perfect lullaby into Jessie Joy's ear about how she has to make her own kind of music and sing her own special song. Even if nobody else sings along.

CHAPTER 45

Takes stubborn to know stubborn

The early morning rays of the August sun warm my brain as I admire the multicolored zinnias that stand three rows deep around our small white house. They're the old-fashioned variety, *zinnia elegans*, that Mama and the butterflies like best. Every spring since I can remember, I've watched Mama twist and turn a maple twig into the red clay, drop a seed into the hole, cover it with dirt, and then pour water all around it from a rusty bucket. And that was that—she forgot about them—but a month later, sturdy green plants pulled flowers out of nowhere, yellow, pink, white, red, violet, gold, and purple.

Daddy bends over the engine of my blue Beetle and pulls the dipstick out for the third time. He sees me staring and shrugs his shoulders. Mama comes out of the house carrying her old dented lunchbox. It's the first S & H Green Stamp prize she ordered from the catalog. It only cost one book of stamps, so she got one for her and one for daddy to carry to the mill. She hands me the man-sized aluminum lunchbox. "Made you some chicken and biscuits and a thermos of iced tea in case you get hungry."

"Thanks, Mama." I put it in the passenger seat.

"Miller, will you get that typewriter from the living room?"

"Aye, Captain," he salutes her and walks to the house.

Mama looks at me, brow furrowed, as if I'm climbing onto a Conestoga wagon bound for Oregon instead of hopping into my cute little car headed toward a brightly burning future. "Don't worry, Mama. I'll be fine."

"Of course you'll be fine. God looks out for the stubborn."

"Takes stubborn to know stubborn," I say, feeling bold as a sunflower.

But as I stare into Mama's hazel eyes, I remember all those times she bought weird stuff I asked for like Roman Meal bread because I thought it would make me lose weight—and Dannon yogurt because I thought it would turn me into a skinny Scandinavian beauty—and all those tubes of Clearasil, even though I've only had about three major pimples in my life. Now, she's smiling at me, as if she'd read my mind. My bottom lip starts trembling when I realize I won't see her until Christmas. She wraps her arms around me and squeezes me tight, her whole life roaring through my arteries.

Finally, she releases me, and we stand in the front yard, breathing the swampy South Carolina air, listening to the hooting and hollering going on across the street as the magnificent Bridges boys pitch horseshoes with Brenda Sulley, the skinny, bucktoothed girl from Knoxville who spends a week with her aunt every year. But Brenda's visit is vastly different this year. Her puffy breasts and the miracle of orthodontics have given this thirteen-year-old girl tremendous power over my twelve-year-old brothers, which proves that sex, like gravity cannot be underestimated.

"Your sister's getting ready to leave," Mama hollers across the street, and then walks toward the house, leaving goodbye unsaid like any sane person.

As Noah and Joshua race across the street, I drink in the sight of their long skinny torsos and freckled faces. Now they're staring at me with their green-flecked eyes. "Okay, munchkins, I'm off to see the Wizard."

Noah looks down at the ground, rocking on his heels, but Joshua throws his sweaty arms around me and squeezes me tight. I'm flabbergasted by how emotional he is—and how strong he is. But I manage to pry myself away from his grip. "See you, Kiddo," I say, then kiss his forehead.

"Later, Tater," he says and runs to the house.

Noah stares at the ground, his toes digging into the red clay dust. I rub my hand across his prickly head. He looks at me, his eyes bewildered at being left alone with his nemesis. I tug on his earlobe. "How about a little whirl before I go?"

He turns his back to me. I grab him under the arms and start twirling him around and around. He squeals like a piglet. He's at least ten pounds heavier than the last time I did this—but I keep twirling him—getting dizzier and dizzier with each turn until I lose my balance and find myself sprawled on the ground beside him, laughing hysterically, tears streaming down my cheeks. The salty taste of my tears and the smell of grass give me that woebegone feeling I used to get after Mama spanked me with a switch from the forsythia bush for some heinous act or another.

I stand and grab Noah's hand, pulling him to his feet. "Come on, little man. Don't take any crap from Joshua—but don't become a bully either."

"Okay, okay," he says, rolling his eyes, then gives me a quick hug and runs to the house.

Daddy shuffles down the porch steps carrying my new Royal Safari portable typewriter with deluxe carrying case that Mama and Gloria Jean purchased with thirty-seven books of S & H green stamps they'd been saving for a year. I open the trunk and Daddy wedges the case between two boxes. Then he opens my car door, and I slide into the driver's seat.

"Close your eyes and open your hand."

I do as I'm told. He places something furry in my hand. I open my eyes. Resting in my palm is that raggedy, purple rabbit's foot that's been missing for years. "Where did you find this?"

"In the cedar chest with my AA stuff. I figure a good luck charm might come in handy," he says repeating what he said when he gave it to me before the South Carolina Spelling Bee—the same thing I said when I gave it back to him before he went to Winding Springs for treatment.

"Thanks, you old coot." I put the heirloom in my pocket.

"I ain't old," he says and kisses my cheek. "I am bold."

I start the car and back out into the street.

"Be good," he hollers.

I cruise past two houses before I look in the rearview mirror and see Daddy standing at the end of our driveway, waving goodbye. He pitched a fit about me driving to Massachusetts, but lost the battle after two friends invited me to stop and spend the night with them along the way. He plotted out the eight hundred and eighty-eight mile trip and wrote two pages of instructions because I'm lousy at reading maps.

I stop at the intersection at Highway 200, remembering how Billy Ray and I sat at this intersection last August—our hearts blazing and "Oh Happy Day" blaring on the radio. I had to sit on my hands to keep them off that handsome, spicy-smelling sailor. I turn north and drive past Kentucky Fried Chicken and Dodge Country, but up ahead at the Esso Station, Gourd is waving for me to stop. We said our goodbyes last night when I filled up the tank, but I pull in anyway. He walks over, almost scowling, and hands me a paper sack. I open it and see it's filled with whopper-sized Atomic fireballs. "Thought these might keep you awake on your trip north," he says.

Tears well in my eyes as I look into the sad face of my hippie friend—both of us remembering the boy who knew I loved fireballs. We mumble our goodbyes. I head north and plop one into my mouth. The hot cinnamony taste takes me back to that day last August when I sat in the front seat of the white Pontiac, and we smooched each other for all we were worth.

I miss everything about Billy Ray. The stubble on his cheek, his warm caramel voice, his soft lips, and dazed topaz eyes—the WHOLE PACKAGE OF HIM—especially that kudzu-that's-just-been-rained-on scent of his that makes me want to scream for a thousand years. But today, I am leaving this town. And the *way* I am leaving feels right.

Billy Ray would be proud of me.

I am proud of myself.

My head is clear—my heart on fire.

Acknowledgements

Hip-hip-hooray to Cathy Smith Bowers, my homey and literary genius, who read draft after draft, determined to see this baby get born. And to Elizabeth Swann and Dannye Romine Powell, for reading several drafts and sharing their brilliant ideas. I am also grateful to Ann Wicker, Richard Krawiec, Sharon Frazier, Rebecca Haworth, Ellen Kelly Smith, Claire Iannini, Grace Morales, and Merrio Barton for reading drafts of this book and offering insightful comments.

A special thanks to Rebecca Haworth, Jennifer Halls, and Kathleen Schneider, for weekly infusions of energy. I'd also like to thank Erin Hubbs for the splendid cover photo and the photo of my mother. Thanks to my son David for the author's photo and for his constant encouragement. Blessings to my students and colleagues at UNCC and everyone else who encouraged me while I wrote this book.

I applaud every member of the Gleaton, Luddy, and Bowman families for their love, support, and guidance, especially my brothers and sisters. I am forever grateful to Charlotte Bowman, my creative genius of a daughter, who twenty years ago *insisted* I was an artist and that I better get busy creating meaningful work to share with others. Her artwork is a constant inspiration.

And ten thousand kudos to Tom Luddy, for lightening my heart and spicing up every one of my days.

About the Cover

Six months after my first novel *Spelldown* was published, my friend Erin Hubbs emailed a photograph of a handsome teenage boy and a cute tweenage girl sitting on opposite sides of a spewing fountain. My flesh broke out in goosebumps when I read the caption, *Karlene and Billy Ray Sighting*. Had my photographer friend stalked down two young characters from my novel like a paparazzi and captured the chemistry between them with her camera? But then another notion fluttered in my heart like a velvet-throated hummingbird. Maybe Karlene and Billy Ray had gone rogue on ME, their so-called author—and now lived happily in the MINDS of READERS where they could pop up, unannounced, at any time, in any place—even at a fountain in Charleston, where Erin immediately recognized them and took their picture.

Author's Note

Readers inspire me. Readers like the woman who called from Jamaica to say Billy Ray Jenkins had stolen her heart and that I should give him a bigger role in my next book. Readers like Mr. James, Mama's sweetheart, who eagerly anticipated more kissing scenes and kept asking me about my progress. And young readers like Michael from Lacy, Washington, who asked: *How come Karlene cusses so much at the beginning of the story, but barely does at the end?* Then there is Paul, who sent an email regarding *Spelldown* that made my heart sing Glory Hallelujah!

> *I have fathered three girls and this is one of the first books I've read—maybe the first—which depicts a real girl who even owns a body (scandal). The absence of the body from most of these books is weird, but you kind of get used to it and I didn't even notice it until I read Spelldown—a book about a real girl with a real body as well as emotions and thoughts. I'm so happy the editorial censors didn't ruin this book.*

But here at the bittersweet end, it has been the Dead who motivated me to weave six years of work into a decent novel. Frances Robertson Gleaton, my profound mother and greatest teacher, died on April 15, but that woman would not let me rest. Every time I doubted my ability to complete this project, she whispered, *"You were born to write this book."* She had said the same thing about my first novel, so I took her at her word.

225

Karon Luddy

photo by Erin Hubbs
Frances Robertson Gleaton
Lancaster County Library, 2007

The day after my mother died, I came across a photo I had never seen of me and my precious niece, Paula, standing beside a white Galaxie 500 Ford. I was dressed in a sailor-collared jumpsuit and spiffy red Keds, and my little niece's face was all scrunched up, as if I had been pinching the back of her neck. I felt shaken by the innocence of the photograph and knew it was a psychic wormhole to the past, but my mother had just died, and I was incapable of delving into the mystery then.

Five months later when I sat down to write the dedication for *Bewilderment of Boys,* the memory of a lovely thirteen-year-old boy returned to me and transported me all the way back to a party on a cold Friday night in December 1967. We are thirteen, the boy and I playing spin the bottle with our friends in the clubhouse at the golf course of our hometown. He spins the bottle, it points to me, and we walk outside into the cold winter night. And by the light of the full moon we face each other. His face so well lit I can see the mole on his left cheek. I shiver being so close to this gorgeous boy. I tell him I am cold. He says he can fix that and whisks his palms together as if they were kindling. Then he frames my face with his warm hands and kisses me tenderly with his luscious lips, bringing moonlight to mine.

That wonderful boy was David Faulkenberry.

Six months later, on the eve of David's fourteenth birthday, a friend accidentally pulled the trigger of a supposedly unloaded gun and David was killed. I had been out of town when it happened—I don't remember where—and had not heard about his death. Somehow I came home on the day of his funeral and discovered the terrible news. How I got to that service is still a mystery. Maybe someone dropped me off at the church. Maybe I took a taxi. Maybe I walked. All I remember is sitting in a red brick church filled with immeasurable grief—feeling like an alien from another galaxy.

Karon Luddy

Karon Gleaton, Paula Williams, 1968

David's spirit continued to visit me as I tried to wrap up this novel. Several times a day, I pulled out the photograph of my fourteen-year-old self and stared at it, looking for clues, trying to remember the occasion. I desperately wanted to connect with David's family. I knew he had an older sister named Hilda, whom I had never met. I found her on Facebook and emailed her, introducing myself as a writer, who was finishing up my second novel, and that I wanted to dedicate the book to David.

Hilda called that afternoon, and we had a joyous, tearful conversation about life and death and first kisses. We also talked about her younger brother Jeff, who had been five-years-old when David died. A flurry of emails passed between the three of us, sharing stories about our lives then and now. Jeff was delighted to hear about that first sweet kiss David and I shared, but it made him ache for the big brother he had lost. I also learned from Hilda that David had died on June 14, 1968.

Later that day, I noticed *July 1968* was date-stamped on the photo and then remembered how film processing was done by mail and usually took two weeks to receive the photos. Suddenly, my memory of that day became crystal clear. That photo of my niece and me had been taken at my sister's house in Kershaw the *morning before* David's funeral—and that poor fourteen-year-old girl had no idea she would be attending the funeral of her first kissable boy that afternoon.

David Faulkenberry 1968

When I was fourteen, I had not known *how* to grieve. Maybe that's why David had showed up in my life again. It was time to mourn and honor his death. But then I remembered how tortured I had felt while writing about

229

the tragic death of the young man in *Bewilderment of Boys* as if I had really *known* him. Perhaps writing this book finally allowed me to grieve David's death.

A week after my conversation with Hilda, I received a photograph of David. When I saw that mole of his was exactly where I remembered it being all those years ago—smack dab in the middle of his left cheek—my heart shattered. For several weeks, I took long walks to contemplate the sweet innocence of our relationship and his early death. Then one day it dawned on me that David and I understood each other perfectly back then and perhaps *still* understood each other perfectly because for some uncanny reason, I felt he had walked in my shoes all these many years, and I had flown with his wings.

Today, I see four distinct blessings from our encounter:

1) David and I shared the same coordinates that night.

2) Our romantic lives took root in holy ground.

3) I lived to tell the story and connected with David's sweet family.

4) You get to hear a story about a marvelous boy you never knew.

In fact, the whole thing is a miracle—one of those spread out kind I rarely notice.

Karon G. Luddy
April 15, 2014

About the Author

photo by David Luddy

Karon Luddy grew up in Lancaster, SC and lives in Charlotte, NC with her husband Tom. She is the award-winning author of the novel *Spelldown* published by Simon and Schuster and *Wolf Heart*, a book of poetry, published by Clemson University Press. She has taught writing intensive classes at the University of North Carolina-Charlotte since 2005. She admits to having a contagion of feeling for writers, readers, and literature. In January 2014, Luddy created Backbone Books and became an independent publisher and author. *Bewilderment of Boys* is her second novel and a sequel to *Spelldown*, her award-winning debut novel.

ALSO BY KARON LUDDY

Spelldown: The Big-Time Dreams of a Small-town Word Whiz

"A resonant, applause-worthy work of fiction.
Readers will revel in the heroine's much-heralded public victories.
Her private triumphs are even more moving and memorable."
Publisher's Weekly starred review

"Artfully glossed with the emerging feminism of the late 1960s.
"This spelldown will have readers spellbound."
Kirkus Reviews starred review

"Luddy's debut novel reveals the roller coaster of adolescence with humor,
caring and an infectious zeal for learning new words."
Parents' Choice Silver Award

"Celebrates the music of the era, the flavor of the South, and
the magic of words to empower young people."
School Library Journal

"A gem of a coming of age story."
Creative Loafing

For more information, please visit
www.karonluddy.com
or email Karon at karonluddy@gmail.com